torical
rthur

First edition published in 2009

Paperback ISBN 9781904312505
Published in the UK by MX Publishing
335 Princess Park Manor, Royal Drive, London, N11 3GX
www.mx-publishing.co.uk

This book is dedicated to my wife (my own Mary Morstan) and to the memory of Pippa

Contents

About the author

Alistair Duncan is an I.T. Consultant and Sherlock Holmes enthusiast. Since the early 1980s he has been a fan of the Great Detective and in February 2008 he released his first book *Eliminate the Impossible* which was a look at the Sherlock Holmes stories and films. He is a member of the Sherlock Holmes Society of London and a member of the Conan Doyle (Crowborough) Establishment.

He lives with his wife in South London.

Acknowledgements

I would like to formally acknowledge the following:

Steve Ball, Catherine Cooke (Sherlock Holmes Collection: Marylebone Library, Westminster Libraries), Phil Cornell (Vice-President of the Sydney Passengers), Christine Corner et al. (Croydon Local Studies Library), Crystal Palace Library, John Hickman, Roger Johnson (Sherlock Holmes Society of London), Brian Pugh and Paul Spiring (authors of Bertram Fletcher Robinson – A Footnote to the Hound of the Baskervilles).

Efforts have been made to identify material still under copyright and seek permission for use. If I have overlooked any item the copyright holder is asked to contact the publisher so that the matter can be rectified in any future edition of this book.

Cover design by Staunch with central illustration by Phil Cornell.

Foreword

Of the dozen or so guides to Sherlock Holmes's London there are two that I recommend to visitors: Arthur Alexander's *Hot on the Scent* and Thomas Wheeler's *Finding Sherlock's London*. Now, thanks to Alistair Duncan, I'll have to add a third.

The point being that the three books complement each other. Mr Alexander offers thirty-five walking tours, all within an area stretching from Whitechapel in the east to Kensington in the west, and all enhanced with anecdote and description. Mr Wheeler deals with each story separately, directing the traveller to the nearest Underground station to each site, and pithily summarising the essential details.

Mr Duncan takes a different approach, as the subtitle of this book indicates. Most importantly, it is, I think, the first of its kind to give equal emphasis to those places associated with Arthur Conan Doyle. We may have wondered why so many of Sherlock Holmes's cases took him south of the Thames, but Alistair Duncan makes all clear: that was the part of London that his creator knew best.

Reading *Close to Holmes* we feel that we are in the company of a knowledgeable, enthusiastic and witty friend. He guides us through most, but not all, of Holmesian London. He doesn't follow Irene Adler to St John's Wood, or Charles Augustus Milverton to Hampstead, but perhaps that would have taken us too far from Conan Doyle. On the other hand, in mentioning "The Priory School", an investigation that took place far from the capital, he advances an interesting and, as far as I'm aware, original idea about the location of "Mackleton" in the Peak District.

In any case, I couldn't possibly be unenthusiastic about a book that features a photograph of the beautiful Maude Fealy! (Intrigued? Then read on…)

Roger Johnson
Editor, The Sherlock Holmes Journal

Introduction

One of the great aspects of the Sherlock Holmes stories is that he operated in a world that still, to a certain extent, exists. When it comes to London this is even truer as a large number of the streets and buildings that existed in the time of Holmes still exist today. Some have changed significantly others have not but it is still very much possible to walk those streets and imagine what it might have been like to have walked them at the end of the nineteenth century.

The idea for this book came about when I was writing my first book - *Eliminate the Impossible*. I intended that it should include a section on locations in London with a connection to the stories. However it soon became apparent that this was a project in its own right and consequently it was left out of that book to be included in this volume.

It also seemed appropriate that this work should not limit itself to areas with links to Holmes but that it should also extend itself to his creator Sir Arthur Conan Doyle. As we look at each location we shall not only look at some of its history but we shall also see in what way it was linked to either Holmes or Conan Doyle and we will also look, in some cases, at the theories about these locations in relation to the Holmes stories.

One cannot hope to cover a subject such as this comprehensively and my choice of locations may seem odd to some readers. Many of the locations will be expected as to omit them would have been absurd (Baker Street for example).

Similarly some will be unexpected and where this occurs I hope you will appreciate why they were included and learn something new.

I very much hope that this book illustrates how the London of Conan Doyle and Holmes both has and has not changed and that it also helps you to tread those streets yourself.

Alistair Duncan, London 2009

1

Baker Street

Arguably Baker Street is the ultimate destination for the Sherlock Holmes fan. As most Sherlockians are aware, in the time of Holmes 221b Baker Street did not exist as an address and the part of the street where the Sherlock Holmes museum is situated used to be referred to as Upper Baker Street. Interestingly, in his original manuscript for *A Study in Scarlet*, Conan Doyle described Holmes and Watson as living in Upper Baker Street but changed it to the regular Baker Street prior to publication. Naturally there has been much speculation as to the location of the house that Conan Doyle really had in mind.

Sherlock Holmes Museum at '221b' Baker Street (2007)

The initial reference to Upper Baker Street in the manuscript does lend some weight to the suggestion that Conan Doyle did have the address of the present museum in mind. The house is representative of the period and the layout both inside and out conforms very much (but not totally) to the descriptions provided by Conan Doyle throughout the stories. The museum management's belief that they occupy the 'real' 221b is largely based on these similarities.

However, as with most aspects of Sherlockian study, there are many competing ideas about the location of 221b with some books detailing theories that the actual site is around the 30s[1]. These theories are often based upon the descriptions of the surrounding streets that appear in some of the stories[2]. The problem with any of these theories is that they are destined to remain just that as there are no known notes of Conan Doyle's that detail the exact address. Given that he was partial to inventing addresses and sometimes entire streets it is quite possible that the 221b of the books is an amalgamation of several addresses. This is the easiest explanation for why people believe it to be in so many different places.

In the 1930s Upper Baker Street was absorbed into the main Baker Street and the street numbers were reallocated. As a result number 221 was one of those allocated to Abbey House which was built in 1932. This building, which was occupied by the Abbey National Bank until 2002, is a huge Art Deco

---

[1] For further details on this see *Baker Street By-Ways* by James Edward Holroyd.

[2] *The Empty House* is one of the stories from which many of the location theories are derived.

construction that covers numbers 215 to 229. A commemorative plaque exists on its outside to signify its association (albeit tenuous) with the great detective. As soon as it was renumbered the bank started to receive letters addressed to Sherlock Holmes and they arrived at such a rate that an employee was appointed full time to answer them. The late Richard Lancelyn Green edited a collection of these letters which were published in paperback by Penguin[3].

The plaque on the wall of Abbey House – unveiled by Jeremy Brett on October 7th 1985

Between May and September 1951 Abbey House was also home to the Sherlock Holmes Exhibition which was part of the Festival of Britain.

---

[3] The Penguin book is entitled *Letters to Sherlock Holmes.*

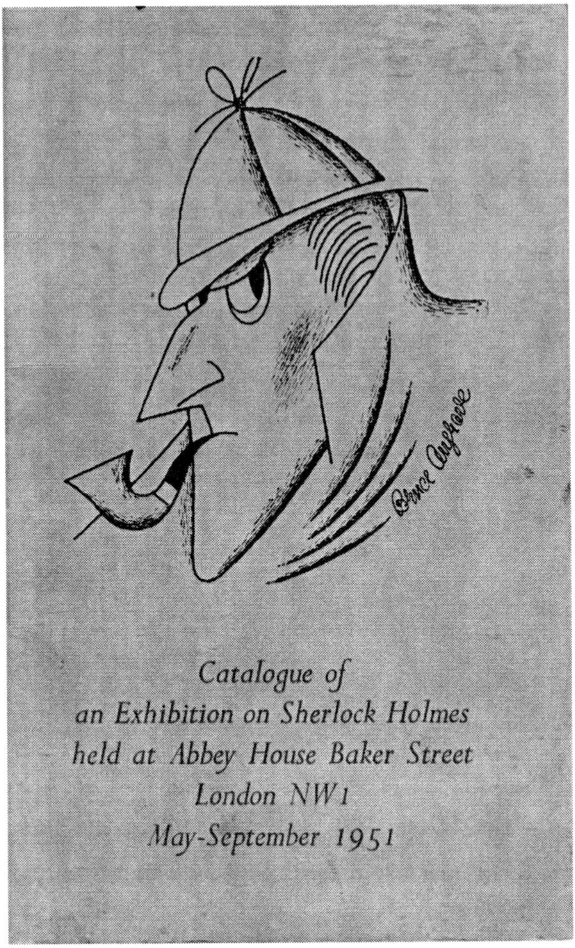

The Catalogue for the 1951 Sherlock Holmes Exhibition (Reproduced with the permission of the Sherlock Holmes Collection: Marylebone Library, Westminster Libraries)

An adult admission ticket for the Sherlock Holmes exhibition (Reproduced with the permission of the Sherlock Holmes Collection: Marylebone Library, Westminster Libraries)

The exhibition consisted of over two hundred items and each of these was listed in the exhibition catalogue. All manner of photographs, paintings, books and letters were featured and many of the items were lent by members of the Conan Doyle family. One of the most notable exhibits was the desk at which Conan Doyle had written many of the Holmes adventures. It was one of the many items that made up the recreation of the sitting room of 221b put together by Michael Weight. Another significant item was a dressing gown which had previously belonged to Sidney Paget, the famous Holmes illustrator, and was lent by Winifred Paget.

The 221b recreation was undoubtedly the centrepiece of the exhibition and after it closed it was purchased by Whitbread who have since had it on display at the Sherlock Holmes Public House (see later). It remained the only recreation of 221b in London until 1990 when the Sherlock Holmes museum opened.

The museum enjoys the distinction of being one of the most successful private museums in the country. Visit on almost any day (the museum is only closed on Christmas Day) and you will find it full of curious visitors posing for photographs seated in Holmes's chair and generally wearing a deerstalker hat. However the chances are that the majority of these visitors will be what might be regarded as casual fans of Holmes rather than serious enthusiasts. The reason for this stems from the fact that the museum generated a considerable amount of controversy both before and after it opened for business. Conan Doyle's daughter, Dame Jean Conan Doyle, was against the museum from the outset. She was very much opposed to the idea of encouraging the belief that her father's famous creation was a real person and knew that the presence of the museum would clearly go contrary to that wish[4].

The other aspect of the museum that excites comment, particularly amongst Sherlockian societies, is the presence of a commemorative blue plaque on the outside which states the building's link with the great detective. At first glance it appears similar to the blue plaques issued by English Heritage but it is not one of theirs and is slightly different in design. The plaque, which was unveiled in the same year that the museum opened, was in fact commissioned by the museum itself.

In 1994 the museum and Abbey House became involved in a dispute over the 221b address. The museum desired to officially renumber itself as 221b and receive Holmes's mail. They lost the argument and had to adopt a different approach. They registered 221b as a company name which allowed them to display the number above the door without any kind of official permission. This was not popular with Westminster City Council but the number remains to this day. Since the Abbey National's

---

[4] Source: 221 Beware (an article by Jean Upton).

departure from Abbey House all mail addressed to 221b has been delivered to the museum.

The ground floor of the museum is free to enter and is dedicated to selling various items to do with Holmes and the Victorian era. It also sells a large number of more general items. Importantly it is from within the shop that the tickets to enter the main museum are purchased. The adjacent door leads to the foot of the steps leading up to the sitting room. The first thing that strikes you, when you reach the top of the stairs and make your way along the landing, is the small size of the sitting room. This is due to the fact that most films inaccurately portray 221b Baker Street as a rather palatial address and thus this is what most people expect to see.

The appearance and layout of the rooms within the museum are broadly accurate and do a very good job of creating the appropriate atmosphere. It has to be said that only the dedicated enthusiast is likely to spot anything overtly amiss and the museum remains the only place in London where you can experience what it might have been like to have lived in Holmes's world.

Aside from Abbey House and the museum there are other Sherlockian areas of interest in the vicinity. In 1999 the Abbey National sponsored the creation of a bronze statue of Sherlock Holmes and this stands outside of the Baker Street Underground station on Marylebone Road. Prior to 1991 there was also a Moriarty's Bar located just inside the entrance to the station but this was forced to close when London Transport introduced a ban on the sale of alcohol on any of its premises.[5]

---

[5] Source: *The Pictorial History of Sherlock Holmes* by Michael Pointer.

The final word on Baker Street must be reserved for the Sherlock Holmes Memorabilia Company which closed in 2006 after fourteen years. It sold a fascinating selection of Holmes related items from key rings to rare editions of the stories. It was also host to an exhibition of the props from the Granada Sherlock Holmes series that starred the late Jeremy Brett. The reason for its position on Baker Street was that it claimed to occupy the site of the 'empty house' from where Colonel Sebastian Moran took aim at what turned out to be a bust of Holmes. It is therefore perhaps fitting that due to rising rents the house is empty once more.

Statue of Sherlock Holmes outside Baker Street Underground Station (2007)

221b Baker Street

Sherlock Holmes

14th October 1988

Dear [redacted]

Mr Holmes thanks you for your letter and has asked me to reply on his behalf.

He regrets that he is unable to comply with your specific request. As you may be aware, Mr Holmes has now retired to Sussex where he spends his time reviewing the records of his cases and keeping bees.

In his own words, Mr Holmes has given himself up entirely "to that soothing life of nature for which I had so often yearned during the long years spent amid the gloom of London."

He is nevertheless, delighted to be the recipient of such vast amounts of mail every week and sends you his cordial regards.

Yours sincerely

[redacted] [redacted]

Nikki [redacted]
Secretary to Sherlock Holmes

The Secretary to Sherlock Holmes,
Abbey National Building Society, 221b Baker Street, London.

Example of a letter sent by the Abbey National in response to a request for Holmes's assistance

Upper Wimpole Street to Regent Street

Upper Wimpole Street and Wimpole Street run parallel to Harley Street and, as with that famous street, they are dominated by medical practices. The streets are named after Wimpole Hall in Cambridgeshire which was owned by the Harley family who gave their name to neighbouring Harley Street.

The door of number 2 Upper Wimpole Street (2008)

Wimpole Street first came into being in around 1724 and from the early 1800s it became popular with doctors as did

Harley Street and Queen Anne Street (see later). However Wimpole Street soon became the street of choice for opticians and dentists. Number one Wimpole Street is the home of the Royal Society of Medicine which moved to the location in 1912 and the street's dental connections are strengthened by the presence of both the British Dental Association and the General Dental Council.

What makes these streets of interest to the fan of Conan Doyle is the fact that number two Upper Wimpole Street was home for a few months to Conan Doyle's short-lived ophthalmic practice.

A close up of the plaque erected by Westminster City Council (2008)

Conan Doyle lived a relatively short distance away in Montague Place (see later). He had been living there since March

1891 and travelled each day on foot to his consulting rooms in Upper Wimpole Street.

Unfortunately it is a matter of record that his practice was a disaster from a medical standpoint as not one patient set foot through the door during the entire time he leased the property. On the other hand this was a godsend from a literary standpoint as it gave him the time to devote to his fledgling writing career.

Only a short time after setting up in Upper Wimpole Street, Conan Doyle sent his agent the manuscript for *A Scandal in Bohemia.* He wrote in his diary on April 3rd 1891 that he had submitted the manuscript, signed it at the end and had given his address as 2 Upper Wimpole Street[6].

The fact that he did so on this and other correspondence was fortunate as there was later to be some considerable confusion over where his ophthalmic practice had actually been. This confusion was caused by none other than Conan Doyle himself.

In August 1892, after his move from Montague Place to South Norwood (see later), Conan Doyle gave an interview to the *Strand Magazine* in which he briefly described the time that he became interested in ophthalmic medicine and how he came to open a practice in Upper Wimpole Street. However by the time he wrote his autobiography his memory of events appeared to have changed. He described himself as occupying rooms at 2 Devonshire Place which is the next street up from Upper Wimpole Street.

Inevitably his word was taken seriously by later researchers and most biographies that followed repeated the Devonshire Place address. Unfortunately the more it was repeated the more

---

[6] Source: The booklet *Conan Doyle of Wimpole Street* by Richard Lancelyn Green.

accepted it became. Richard Lancelyn Green's booklet on the subject states that in June 1950 the first attempts were made to get a plaque erected at 2 Devonshire Place to commemorate Conan Doyle's time there and the fact that the earliest Sherlock Holmes short stories were written there.

These requests were refused on the grounds that Conan Doyle had not actually lived at the address or spent considerable time working there. Further requests were made in the years that followed but over a decade later there had been no success. However there was success elsewhere. Conan Doyle's former house at 12 Tennison Road, South Norwood received a blue plaque in 1973[7] (see later).

A few further attempts were made to get a plaque erected at the Devonshire Place address but it was not until July 7th 1980, the fiftieth anniversary of Conan Doyle's death, that the lack of a plaque was brought to the fore by *The Daily Telegraph.* Nine years later the Arthur Conan Doyle Society was founded and four years after this the society decided to sponsor the erection of the long awaited plaque. During the process the information about the correct Upper Wimpole Street address came to light and in 1994 the plaque was finally erected in the proper place.

Queen Anne Street connects Harley Street with Wimpole Street and was a street which many medical practices over spilled into. Doctor Watson describes himself as being resident here in 1902 during the events described in *The Illustrious Client.*

---

[7] Source: English Heritage.

Queen Anne Street (heading west) as seen from Harley Street (2008)

One of the many debates amongst Sherlockian scholars is the reason for Watson moving here and away from Baker Street. The two prevailing theories are that Watson had either married again or that he had been forced back to work due to his gambling debts[8]. The ammunition for the latter argument comes from *Shoscombe Old Place* in which Watson refers to spending half his wound pension on racing and *The Dancing Men* in which Holmes refers to Watson's cheque book being locked away in his own drawer. To the present author the marriage theory is more plausible as Watson's marriage is referred to in *The Blanched Soldier* which was written two years after *The Illustrious Client*.

---

[8] Source: *A Sherlock Holmes Commentary* by D. Martin Dakin

This is a wider view of Upper Wimpole Street. Number 2 is the second door from the right (2008)

The Langham Hotel, which is a walk of a few minutes from Queen Anne Street, can make four immediate claims on the interest of the Sherlock Holmes or Conan Doyle enthusiast. On August 30th 1889 Conan Doyle attended a dinner at the hotel at the invitation of J. M. Stoddart, the editor of *Lippincott's Monthly Magazine*. Among the other guests at this dinner was none less than Oscar Wilde. Conan Doyle himself regarded it as a 'golden evening' and by the end of the dinner he had been commissioned by Stoddart to write what became his second Sherlock Holmes story *The Sign of Four* (1890). Wilde also received a commission and subsequently wrote his only novel *The Picture of Dorian Gray* which was published in the same year as Conan Doyle's novel.

The memory of the evening was certainly still in Conan Doyle's mind when he wrote the early part of his story as Captain Morstan, the father of Holmes's client Mary Morstan, is described as staying at the Langham ten years prior to the events of the story. The final two references to the hotel are made in *A Scandal in Bohemia* and *The Disappearance of Lady Frances Carfax*. In the former the King of Bohemia stays at the Langham under an assumed name and in the latter the hotel is used by the Honourable Philip Green during his London stay.

The hotel was opened by the Prince of Wales (the future King Edward VII) in 1865 having been built over the course of the previous two years. It cost a significant £300,000 to build and, at the time it opened, was the most modern hotel of the time. One of its claims to fame was that it was the first hotel in England to have hydraulic lifts. In addition it was one of the earliest to make use of electricity having its porch lit by this method as early as 1879. In 1870 an American called James Sanderson was appointed General Manager and under his stewardship the hotel began to attract a large American clientele.

Among the most notable of these was the author Mark Twain. It is therefore not surprising that Stoddart chose this hotel at which to hold his dinner with Conan Doyle and Wilde.

The King of Bohemia visits Holmes and Watson. Of all the characters that Conan Doyle had stay at the Langham the King was the most illustrious.

The hotel also attracted famous people from other countries. In addition to Conan Doyle and Wilde it attracted the custom of Napoleon III (who spent much of his enforced exile from France at the hotel[9]) and, in later years, Noel Coward.

---

[9] Source: Langham Hotel Website.

Conan Doyle's repeated use of the Langham Hotel does raise an interesting question. Why was he content to name this hotel when he was so reticent about naming others? In later stories such as *The Blue Carbuncle*, *The Noble Bachelor* and *The Hound of the Baskervilles* he referred to hotels but always did so ambiguously either avoiding the mention of a name at all or providing a false one. We shall revisit this question and some possible explanations in our look at the hotels on Northumberland Avenue.

During the Second World War the Langham was closed to the public due to bomb damage although it was used by the BBC for staff and guests. In 1965 the BBC bought the Langham outright and somc of its radio broadcasts were performed from the building.

However the BBC did not retain ownership of the Langham. It was sold in 1986, with the blessing of English Heritage, and a massive refurbishment project was started with the aim of making it a working hotel once more. In 1991 this was completed (at a cost of £100 million) and the hotel reopened. It immediately returned to its old habit of attracting royalty and the rich and famous and is now the flagship hotel of Langham Hotels International.

The Langham Hotel (2008)

Woodcut of the Langham Hotel c1880

Regent Street to Pall Mall

Regent Street is one of London's premier retail streets. It was named after the then Prince Regent (later King George IV) and was designed by John Nash (1752 – 1835). It begins just south of Langham Place, the site of the Langham Hotel and All Souls Church (also designed by Nash). It crosses over Oxford Street and continues south towards Piccadilly where it crosses over Piccadilly Circus finally terminating when it connects to Pall Mall.

Regent Street c1880

As the fan of Sherlock Holmes will know it is down this street that Holmes and Watson follow a cab as it tails Sir Henry Baskerville and Dr Mortimer on their way back to the Northumberland Hotel after their visit to Holmes in Baker Street. This scene was one of many illustrated by Sidney Paget and it has its own interesting story. According to *Baker Street By-Ways* by James Edward Holroyd, the illustration has always been printed the wrong way round in English editions of the story.

Holmes and Watson are spotted as they follow the cab carrying Stapleton down Regent Street in The Hound of the Baskervilles – The illustration is shown here the correct way round.

There are a number of indications that this is indeed the case. If you look at the illustration as printed in any English edition it is plain to see that Watson's morning-coat is buttoned right over left when it should be the opposite. Holroyd's suggested explanation for this is that the image was destined to appear on an even numbered page when printed and the convention was to have characters facing inwards towards the spine. Regardless of which way round the picture is shown it is rather curious to note that Holmes and Watson are ahead of the cab they are supposed to be tailing. No doubt this was done to ensure their prominence in the illustration.

However this is not the only connection that Regent Street and some of the neighbouring streets have with the Great Detective. Conduit Street connects with Regent Street just south of Oxford Circus. It is an unremarkable road but its claim to fame from a Sherlockian perspective is that it was home to the man described by Holmes as the second most dangerous man in London – Colonel Sebastian Moran[10].

Slightly further down Regent Street we find the site of the former Café Royal. This restaurant, sadly shut down in December 2008 after one hundred and fifty years, was the favourite establishment of the literary set in the late nineteenth century with Oscar Wilde as one of its most famous patrons[11].

---

[10] Source: *The Empty House*

[11] According to the BBC the Café Royal was the site of the only cordial meeting between Oscar Wilde and the Marquess of Queensbury before the latter accused Wilde of being a homosexual. It was Wilde's decision to launch a libel prosecution that ultimately led to his own trial and conviction.

For the Sherlockian the connection lies in the adventure *The Illustrious Client* where it is outside the Café that Holmes is assaulted by thugs in the pay of Baron Gruner. After carrying out their task they escape through the café into Glasshouse Street which lies behind.

Regent Street (2008)

John Nash – designer of Regent Street

Conduit Street, home to Colonel Moran (2008)

The Café Royal, a few months before its closure (2008)

Glasshouse Street – Holmes's attackers escaped down this road in The Illustrious Client (2008)

A couple of minutes further down Regent Street bring you to Piccadilly Circus where we find a pivotal location in the Sherlock Holmes stories – the Criterion.

The Criterion Theatre and Restaurant are built on the site formerly occupied by an Inn called the White Bear. This was a well regarded coaching inn and thrived during the 18th century but the passing of the coaching era led to it being demolished in 1870[12]. The lease for the site was granted to the wine merchants Spiers & Pond and they organised a competition to find an architect to design a restaurant and tavern. There were fifteen entries but the contract was eventually awarded to Thomas Verity (1837 – 1891) and he promptly founded his own architectural practice which still trades today under the name Verity and Beverley.

---

[12] Source: Criterion Theatre Website

Criterion Theatre entrance (2008)

Piccadilly Circus 1902 – The Criterion is to the right but out of shot

Building began in 1871 and was completed two years later. The restaurant and bar opened in November 1873 and the accompanying theatre in March 1874. The play with which it opened had its debut performance on March 21st and was entitled *An American Lady*. According to the New York Times the performance was not without incident. The play had been booked out long in advance and the pit area was overcrowded to such an extent that the resulting discomfort suffered by the audience led to angry scenes and the curtain came down very soon after it had first risen without anyone uttering a line. Order was eventually restored and the leading lady was presented with a great many bouquets at the end of the performance.

The Criterion Bar is where Watson sets his first foot on the path to meeting Sherlock Holmes. As described in *A Study in Scarlet*, it is here that Watson bumps into Stamford who was a former dresser (or junior doctor) under him at St Bartholomew's Hospital. During a subsequent lunch together at the Holborn restaurant Holmes's name is discussed (see later) and they later travel to the hospital to meet him. The rest, as they say, is history.

According to several sources *A Study in Scarlet*, published in December 1887, is set in 1881[13]. This is interesting as it means that the most famous landmark in the immediate area would not have been present at the time the events of the story took place or the date when it was published. Namely this is the statue outside the Criterion, often referred to as *The Angel of Christian Charity* but generally known as *Eros*, which was erected in 1893.

---

[13] *A Sherlock Holmes Commentary* by D. Martin Dakin and *The New Annotated Sherlock Holmes* by Leslie Klinger both agree on this date.

The entrance to the Criterion Restaurant (2008) – the entrance to the theatre is the other side of Lillywhites which can be just seen on the right. Note that the opening date is shown as 1874 which is at odds with the Criterion official website.

Pall Mall

Pall Mall c1910 looking towards Trafalgar Square – The Reform Club is the second building from the right

Pall Mall is the area of London in which you find a great number of the private members clubs that have historically been frequented by nobility and politicians. One of the most notable was the Carlton Club[14], arguably a second home of the Conservative Party, which was founded in 1832 and relocated to

[14] Sir James Damery from *The Illustrious Client* was a member of the Carlton Club.

Pall Mall in 1835. It remained there until the building was destroyed in an air raid during the Second World War.

The Reform Club can be seen on the left of this picture, immediately behind the van (2008)

Despite the departure of the Carlton Club a large number of other clubs still call the area home. Conan Doyle was himself a member of three of the clubs in Pall Mall. The first was the Reform Club[15] of which Conan Doyle was a member from June 1892. The second was the Athenaeum of which he became a member in March 1901[16]. Finally, the third was the Royal

---

[15] Source: *Conan Doyle: The Man Who Created Sherlock Holmes* by Andrew Lycett.

[16] As above.

Automobile Club, founded in 1897, which opened for business in Pall Mall in March 1911 having relocated from Piccadilly. Conan Doyle became a member in 1903[17] soon after buying his first car.

The Athenaeum Club at 107 Pall Mall (2006)

The Athenaeum is of particular interest as it was a club that had been specifically set up in 1824 with the idea of having scientific, artistic and literary minds amongst its members. It cannot have been lost on Conan Doyle when he was elected a member that his great literary hero Sir Walter Scott had also been a member. Conan Doyle's famous contemporary fellow members included Winston Churchill, Rudyard Kipling and Cecil Rhodes who died one year after Conan Doyle was elected.

---

[17] Source: *Conan Doyle: The Man Who Created Sherlock Holmes* by Andrew Lycett.

Turning to the Holmes connection, it was also on Pall Mall that the Diogenes Club, co-founded by Mycroft Holmes, was based. In *The Greek Interpreter* Holmes first speaks to Watson about his brother and explains that Mycroft lives in Pall Mall opposite the club which he helped to found. Mycroft's connection to Pall Mall is also mentioned in the stories *The Bruce-Partington Plans* and *The Final Problem.* These are not the only connections however. Watson travels to a letting Agent in Pall Mall during *The Solitary Cyclist* in an attempt to gain information about the tenant of Charlington Hall. Finally, in *The Abbey Grange*, Holmes and Watson visit the shipping office of the Adelaide-Southampton Line, at the end of Pall Mall, in order to obtain information about Captain Crocker.

Mycroft Holmes co-founder of the Diogenes Club from The Greek Interpreter

Although Conan Doyle himself never stated it the suggestion has been made by many that the Diogenes Club was little more than a front for the British Secret Service with Mycroft as its head. This inference is largely drawn from *The Bruce-Partington Plans* where Mycroft is responsible for involving Holmes in the case which concerns '...the most jealously guarded of all government secrets.'

However such a lofty position seems unlikely when you bear in mind Holmes's description of his own brother in the same story as a man who remains a subordinate and has no ambitions of any kind.

An etching of Raeburn's portrait of Sir Walter Scott (1771 – 1832) literary great and one time member of the Athenaeum

Northumberland Avenue and its hotel mysteries

Northumberland Avenue and the surrounding area are mentioned in several of the Sherlock Holmes stories. In *The Illustrious Client* we learn that Holmes and Watson frequented a Turkish Bath situated near the avenue (close to the present day Sherlock Holmes public house) and the avenue is also mentioned in regards to its many hotels.

One of the references to a hotel on Northumberland Avenue occurs in *The Noble Bachelor*. In this story, Holmes is able to get on the track of his quarry, Francis Moulton, by using the semi-complete details of a bill (obtained from Inspector Lestrade) to locate his hotel. This hotel, he tells Watson, was on Northumberland Avenue.

The decision on Conan Doyle's part to conceal the identity of the hotel is interesting as he had been perfectly willing to identify the Langham Hotel in *A Scandal in Bohemia* (mentioned earlier) which was published the previous year and before that in *The Sign of Four* (published in 1890). He would later go on to mention the Langham again in the 1911 adventure *The Disappearance of Lady Frances Carfax* and the Charing Cross Hotel in *The Bruce-Partington Plans* (1908). So why was he disinclined to be specific with the hotels on Northumberland Avenue?

In the case of *The Noble Bachelor* the answer may well lie in the fact that Conan Doyle actually stated the prices being charged by the hotel. When Holmes explains to Watson how he had determined that the hotel was on the avenue from the bill he adds that 'there are not many in London which charge at that rate'. He quotes the price as being eight shillings for a bed and eight pence for a glass of sherry[18]. Conan Doyle was well known for not always concerning himself with details and it is quite possible that he came up with these prices based on general hotel experience and not from actually checking them at the hotel in question. Therefore he may have concealed the identity of the hotel in order to avoid being picked up on his potentially inaccurate pricing by the hotel's management.

It is possible to theorise as to the identity of the hotel in question by looking at the text of the story. Holmes explains to Watson that that he deliberately checked the expensive hotels and 'In the second one which I visited in Northumberland Avenue, I learned by an inspection of the book that Francis H. Moulton, an American gentleman, had left only the day before...'

So, right at the beginning, we know that the hotel in question was definitely on the avenue. At the time the three luxury hotels on that road were the Grand, the Metropole and the Victoria. All of these were built in the 1880s, the former two by the Gordon

---

[18] Eight shillings for a bed would have indeed been expensive. According to the website for the Langham Hotel, which was one of Conan Doyle's favoured hotels, they only started charging nine shillings for a room in 1904. This was twelve years after the date *The Noble Bachelor* was published and, according to some sources, sixteen years after the date in which the story was set (1888).

Hotels Company (opened in 1887 and 1885 respectively) and the latter by the imaginatively named Northumberland Avenue Hotel Company[19] (also opened in 1887[20]).

According to hotel historians, all three of these hotels were particularly popular with American visitors. This was partly because of the luxurious conditions they offered and also the ready access to the West End and major rail stations such as Charing Cross. This would therefore fit as the area in which Francis Moulton was likely to stay (being both American and wealthy). Furthermore, as this was a place to which Americans gravitated, it is not unreasonable to suggest that both of the hotels checked by Holmes were on this road. This assumption is not too much of a leap as he already suspected that he was seeking an American and would have known that the hotels in this area were popular with them. If we continue to follow this line of thought and assume that Holmes in his search either walked up the avenue from the south or down from the north the second of these hotels that he would have visited, in either direction, would have been the Victoria[21]. The Victoria was very

---

[19] Source: Ministry of Defence Website.

[20] There is disagreement regarding these dates. According to *The Face of London* by Harold P. Clunn, the Grand was opened in 1880 and the Victoria in 1890. Clunn also maintains that all three hotels were built by the Gordon Hotels Company. The author has been unable to verify which source is correct so both sets of dates are presented for completeness.

[21] Not an unreasonable assumption as Holmes was a logical man and would likely visit the hotels in order rather than randomly.

likely to have been expensive as it had cost £520,000 to build which was double the original estimate[22].

The Victoria had many of the modern conveniences of the time. It was one of the first hotels in the capital to be completely lit by electricity, which came from its own generators, and had lifts serving every floor. However, despite these modern facilities, the hotel was also surprisingly deficient in other areas. Despite having five hundred apartments there were only four bathrooms. Guests who wished to wash in the privacy of their rooms were provided with a shallow portable bath that was filled each morning by the staff with a mere few inches of water.

---

[22] Source: Ministry of Defence Website.

An illustration of the Hotel Victoria from 1904

HOTEL VICTORIA
NORTHUMBERLAND AVENUE, CHARING CROSS, LONDON, W.C.
MOST CENTRALLY SITUATE FOR
ALL LONDON ATTRACTIONS.
BANQUETING-ROOM FOR
PRIVATE PARTIES.
THIS Magnificent Hotel is one of the Finest in the World; 500 Apartments, Public and Private Rooms and Baths, unsurpassed for comfort, convenience, and elegance. Completely lit by Electricity. Passenger Lifts to every Floor.
The Table d'Hote open to Non-Residents.
THE BEST DINNER IN LONDON.
From 6 to 8.30 p.m., price 5s.
SEPARATE TABLES RESERVED FOR LARGE OR SMALL PARTIES.
SPECIAL DINNERS, 6s. 6d., 7s. 6d., and upwards.
Served in either the Public or Private Rooms. For Parties of 6, 8, 10, or more persons.
Telegraphic Address: "VICTORIOLA, LONDON."

Advert for the Hotel Victoria from 1892 (The Illustrated London News) – the same year The Noble Bachelor was published

The former Hotel Victoria (now known, confusingly, as the Grand) at 8 Northumberland Avenue (2008)

Staying with the hotels on Northumberland Avenue, the Hotel Metropole, which was at the southern end of the avenue close to the Embankment, was the location for Conan Doyle's reception celebrating his marriage to Jean Leckie. The wedding took place on September 18th 1907[23] and the reception (which was held in the hotel's Whitehall Rooms) was attended by over two hundred guests including such literary greats as J.M. Barrie

---

[23] The event was reported in the September 19th issue of The Times. Among the guests mentioned in the article were a Mr Sholto Wood and a Dr Edward Musgrave. It is possible that it was from these men that Conan Doyle took the names for his Sholto family of *The Sign of Four* (1890) and for Reginald Musgrave from *The Musgrave Ritual* (1893).

and Bram Stoker[24]. Three years later, in 1910, Conan Doyle stayed at the Metropole when his plays *The House of Temperley* and, later, *The Speckled Band* were playing at the Adelphi Theatre (see later).

---

[24] Arthur Conan Doyle (Crowborough) Establishment 2008 Birthday File

Hotel Metropole c1900

Postcard of the interior of the Hotel Metropole from the early 1900s. It provides an illustration of the surroundings in which Conan Doyle's wedding reception would have taken place.

The Metropole building (2008)

It is unquestionably the case that the most famous story to involve the Northumberland Avenue area and its hotels is *The Hound of the Baskervilles*. Sir Henry Baskerville is described as residing in the Northumberland Hotel but a hotel by this name does not exist. Consequently there has been considerable debate as to which of the actual hotels is the one that Conan Doyle had in mind. We know from Andrew Lycett's recent biography that Conan Doyle had often stayed at three hotels in the area. These were Morley's, The Golden Cross and The Grand[25]. The first of these was in Trafalgar Square, the second on the Strand and the third at the top of Northumberland Avenue. Given the number of times he stayed in these hotels before and around the time of the publication of *The Hound of the Baskervilles* it is not unreasonable to presume that one of them was the model for the Northumberland. However they are by no means the only candidates.

---

[25] The architect of the Grand Hotel, according to *The Story of Charing Cross* by J. Holden Macmichael, was one Mr Alfred Waterhouse. This same man was also the architect of the Natural History Museum in South Kensington.

Grand Hotel (opened in 1887) shown in the early 1900s

One of the other locations put forward as a candidate is the Northumberland Arms Inn[26]. This, which we shall cover later, is now known as the Sherlock Holmes Public House. It seems unlikely that this would be the location of Sir Henry's Hotel. Firstly it is decidedly small and it seems likely that Sir Henry would have stayed in a grander (no pun intended) hotel. You could argue that Sir Henry's farming background might have induced him to lean towards a small and less fancy establishment but the size of the hotel in which he stays can be inferred from a conversation he has regarding his missing boot.

---

[26] Suggested by W. S. Baring-Gould in his *Annotated Sherlock Holmes.*

The Grand Hotel building (2008)

People familiar with the story will know that two of Sir Henry's boots vanish during his brief London stay (although one is later returned). When the second goes missing Sir Henry has an angry exchange with a German waiter working at the hotel. Said waiter informs him that he has made enquiries 'all over the hotel' in an effort to locate the missing boot. To the present author this implies that a large number of people were consulted and by extension a larger establishment. So we should set this unlikely candidate to one side and resume our look at Conan Doyle's three regular haunts.

Golden Cross House. In Conan Doyle's day this was the site of the Golden Cross Hotel (2008)

Golden Cross Hotel in the late 1800s

The only clue as to the Northumberland's location comes from the cabman John Clayton whose cab was used by Stapleton to trail Sir Henry around London. In his interview with Holmes, Clayton reveals that his cab was hailed in Trafalgar Square and then driven down to the hotel. As Stapleton was determined to tail Sir Henry it makes sense to suggest that the relevant hotel and the people entering and leaving it would have been clearly visible from his position in the square until such time as he had engaged his transportation. Had it not been so easy to watch there would have been the chance of Sir Henry leaving the hotel unnoticed. If you accept this suggestion it would largely exclude the Golden Cross Hotel as its main entrance was situated on the Strand and would have been only just visible from the southern side of the square[27].

Furthermore there is additional ammunition against the Golden Cross' chances of being the Northumberland. Holmes reveals that Stapleton stayed in the Mexborough Private Hotel on Craven Street[28]. Following this road north brings you to the

---

[27] As well as its main entrance onto the Strand the Golden Cross Hotel had a rear entrance that faced onto Duncannon Street. This and the fact that the hotel had approximately seventy bedrooms were mentioned in the Times of March 1st 1897.

[28] According to *The Story of Charing Cross* by J. Holden Macmichael, published 1906, there were two hotels on Craven Street. The Craven Hotel was situated at numbers 44 and 46 and at 27 Macmichael mentions the presence of a private hotel. This description is interesting as the same terminology is applied to the Mexborough. According to Jack Tracy's *Encyclopaedia Sherlockiana* a 'private' hotel was not licensed to serve alcohol.

Strand and virtually opposite the site of the Golden Cross Hotel[29]. Had this been the Northumberland it would have been more practical for Stapleton to have hailed his cab from outside Charing Cross Station from where the hotel entrance could be easily observed rather than Trafalgar Square where it would have been difficult. The fact that he chose the latter in which to hail his cab suggests that the Northumberland was closer to that location. This brings us back to Morley's and The Grand.

Craven Street today - the location of Stapleton's hotel. The Golden Cross building can be seen at the end of the road (2008)

---

[29] The Golden Cross Hotel closed in 1930, the same year in which Conan Doyle died. Its closure and the news that the building was to be demolished were reported in the September 22nd issue of the Times.

Trafalgar Square early 1900s. Morley's hotel can be seen on the left across from the Grand.

South Africa House on the site of the former Morley's Hotel (2005)

While it is possible to argue that we have successfully eliminated the Golden Cross it does not help determine definitively which hotel out of the Grand and Morley's is the best candidate as neither has any significant advantage over the others. The sad fact is that, barring some hitherto hidden papers emerging with more details, there is unlikely to ever be a consensus on the subject within the Sherlockian community.

A probable reason for Conan Doyle's ambiguity is similar to that stated for *The Noble Bachelor*. In *The Hound of the Baskervilles* the hotel is shown in a decidedly bad light as an establishment where a guest's possessions can be easily lost. In his summing up of the case, Holmes makes clear his belief that a member of staff was bribed in order that Stapleton could obtain Sir Henry's boot. Sir Henry himself describes the hotel as a 'den of thieves'. You could argue that it is possible that Conan Doyle feared some kind of legal action were he to imply that an existing hotel had such a problem. After all he was, by this time, a man of some considerable fame and influence and there can be little doubt that people who read his story would have been put off the idea of staying at a hotel if they believed it was lacking honest staff.

Returning to one of the earlier candidates, the Sherlock Holmes pub opened under its present name in 1957[30]. Prior to this it had been a small hotel called the Northumberland Arms. Six years earlier, as previously mentioned, the Festival of Britain had taken place and one of the exhibits had been a recreation of the 221b sitting room. The pub's owners Whitbread & Co purchased the

---

[30] According to the official Website.

exhibit and installed it on the first floor alongside the restaurant area.

The management claim a Sherlockian link for the premises by suggesting on their website that it was here that Holmes tracked down Francis Moulton in *The Noble Bachelor*. However their reasoning for this is unknown. As we have already mentioned, Moulton's hotel is described as being in Northumberland Avenue whereas the pub is in Northumberland Street. In the author's opinion this effectively rules it out as a candidate. Curiously they do not restate the theory that they are a candidate for the Northumberland Hotel. This is interesting as you would have expected them to do so if they had any belief that it was the case.

Sherlock Holmes Pub (2007)

The presence of the 221b sitting room naturally makes this an important stop for tourists regardless of whether they are particularly fans of the Sherlock Holmes stories. The layout of the ground floor is interesting in this respect. It has essentially been divided down the middle. The first half (reached through the door on the right in the above picture) is almost devoid of any Holmes related material. The other half, in contrast, contains a vast amount of memorabilia, the principal exhibit being the head of the Baskerville family's canine nemesis. This layout largely has the effect of drawing tourists into the one half of the pub leaving the other half for the locals.

The first floor, which contains the restaurant, has no such split personality. Holmes related memorabilia are on the walls as you travel the staircase and as you make your way to the restaurant reception you are able to view the recreated sitting room through a series of port-holes. Given the limited space given over to the exhibit the end result is impressive. The restaurant itself is not unreasonably priced and the diner can chose from a variety of dishes most of which are named after a Holmes adventure.

The Strand

The Strand is a road with many connections to Sherlock Holmes and Arthur Conan Doyle. This is only fitting as the magazine that made them famous took its name from this very road. Starting at Trafalgar Square it heads east until it connects with Fleet Street, the historic home of newspapers and journalism. Its name derives from the Old English word for shore or river bank.

Bound copy of the Strand Magazine from 1894

The Strand's only rail terminal, Charing Cross Station, opened for business in 1864[31] on the site of the former Hungerford Market, which had closed two years earlier. It provides access to large sections of South London and Kent with most of its trains passing through London Bridge Station on their way. The station was designed by Sir John Hawkshaw (1811 – 1891) who was also responsible for designing Cannon Street station (see later).

Charing Cross Hotel and Station (right). Early 1900s

The Charing Cross Hotel whose façade now obscures the main station was built in the following year and was designed by Edward Middleton Barry (1830 – 1880) whose other significant achievements included the Royal Opera House in Covent Garden. The hotel was an immediate success with over fifty

---

[31] *The Face of London* by Harold P. Clunn.

percent occupancy on its opening day[32]. The replica of the Eleanor Cross was erected in the forecourt during the same year that the hotel opened. The original, which commemorated one of the places where Queen Eleanor – wife of King Edward I – rested on her route to burial, was demolished in 1647 and originally stood in Whitehall. Its former place is now occupied by a statue of King Charles I. This position is recognised as the centre of London and licensed black cab drivers need to know all the streets within a six mile radius of this point. This is what is known as 'the knowledge'.

Sir John Hawkshaw – architect of Charing Cross Station

Charing Cross station and the surrounding area are mentioned in several of the Sherlock Holmes adventures. It is from this station that Irene Adler catches a train bound for the

[32] *The Face of London* by Harold P. Clunn.

continent in *A Scandal in Bohemia* as part of her ultimately successful plan to elude Holmes. The station's waiting room, as Holmes mentions to Watson at the end of *The Empty House*, is where his left canine was knocked out by a man named Mathews.

A face on view of the station and hotel c 1890

It is also from this station that Holmes and Watson travel to Kent to investigate mysteries brought to their attention by Inspector Stanley Hopkins. The first of these trips being to Chatham to investigate the adventure *The Golden Pince-Nez*. The second to travel to the fictional village of Marsham[33] to

[33] A possibility is that the name stems from the village of Marsham in Norfolk. In 1903 Conan Doyle stayed at the Hill House Public House in Happisburgh and while there he wrote *The Dancing Men*. The Literary Norfolk website states that this was a motoring holiday so it is possible that he passed by or through Marsham or perhaps simply saw it on a local map and then decided to use the name in *The Abbey Grange* which was published the following year.

assist in the mystery entitled *The Abbey Grange.* The final connection comes from *The Bruce-Partington Plans* where Holmes arranges the capture of the agent Oberstein in the smoking room of the Charing Cross Hotel.

The Eleanor Cross outside Charing Cross Hotel / Station (2008)

In 1896 Conan Doyle had published *Rodney Stone* a novel that revolved around bare-knuckle boxing during the Regency period. In 1910 he brought it to the stage under the title of *The House of Temperley*[34]. For this purpose he leased the Adelphi theatre at a cost of £600 per week. Unfortunately the play was not a success and closed with four months remaining on the lease. This was largely due to the fact that boxing was illegal at the time and audiences struggled with the idea of watching boxing on the stage. Faced with the potential loss of £9,600 on the lease alone Conan Doyle turned to Sherlock Holmes. Realising that Holmes would draw audiences he quickly dramatised his favourite short story – *The Speckled Band* and had it in rehearsals within weeks. The play opened on June 4th 1910.

H.A. Saintsbury (1869 – 1939) played Holmes and Lyn Harding (1867 – 1952) played Dr Grimsby Roylott. This would not be Harding's only brush with the Great Detective. He would later go on to play Professor Moriarty on screen against Arthur Wontner's Holmes. Harding and Conan Doyle had a difference of opinion about how Roylott should be portrayed. Whereas Conan Doyle wanted very much the conventional and believable villain, Harding wanted to play Roylott larger than life and decidedly melodramatic. This led to strained relations between the two men. These were only solved when J.M. Barrie (1860 – 1937), better known as the author of *Peter Pan*, stepped in. He was a mutual friend and after sitting through a rehearsal of the play he advised Conan Doyle to defer to Harding.

---

[34] Source: *Sherlock Holmes – The Published Apocrypha* by Jack Tracy

Adelphi Theatre, The Strand (2008)

This proved to be the correct decision as Harding's Roylott was a hit with audiences on the opening night. In a considerable show of good grace Conan Doyle sent Harding a congratulatory letter praising his performance. Harding went on to repeat the role on screen opposite Raymond Massey as Holmes in the 1931 film of the same name. Four years after this came the first of his outings as Moriarty against Arthur Wontner.

J. M. Barrie – Author of Peter Pan and friend of Arthur Conan Doyle (c1890)

Turning to restaurants, Holmes and Watson appear to rather have enjoyed dining out and one of the mentioned establishments was Simpson's. This restaurant, which is still in business today, features in *The Dying Detective* and *The Illustrious Client*. In the latter story Holmes and Watson dine there on no less than two occasions.

Simpson's Restaurant (2008)

The site was originally home to the Fountain Tavern which itself was home to an early eighteenth century literary group called The Kit-Cat Club. In 1828 one Samuel Reiss opened the Grand Cigar Divan on the site which became known as a famous cigar and coffee house. It was a club in all but name and gentlemen paid one guinea a year for access to the facilities. One of the most popular pastimes on the site was chess. This practice developed to such an extent that it became known as 'The Home of Chess' and Howard Staunton (1810-1874), the first English world chess champion, was a visitor[35]. Other illustrious visitors over the years included Charles Dickens, George Bernard Shaw and William Gladstone.

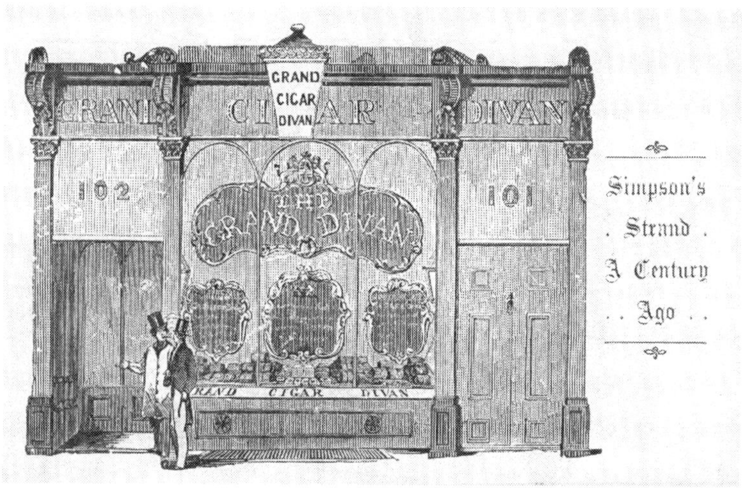

A drawing of The Grand Cigar Divan as it would have appeared at around 1828

In 1848 Samuel Reiss joined forces with caterer John Simpson. The site was subsequently renamed 'Simpson's Grand Divan Tavern'. It specialised in British produce and developed the practice of wheeling joints of meat to the tables to be carved in front of the customer. In the 1890s it was demolished but was

---

[35] Source: Simpsons official Website

rebuilt and opened again in 1900. These dates are interesting as they suggest that Holmes and Watson dined there before and after it was rebuilt. According to a number of sources, *The Dying Detective* was set in 1890 which would have been only a short time before the demolition. *The Illustrious Client* is often stated to have been set in 1902. This means that modern day visitors to the restaurant could well be dining in a building that has changed little since Holmes's last documented visit.

Howard Staunton c1860

Moving from restaurants to hotels, the Savoy Hotel was opened in 1889[36] and is still today one of London's most prestigious hotels. The architect was Thomas Edward Collcutt (1840 – 1924) who was also responsible for the design of the Palace Theatre in Cambridge Circus. The most famous manager of the hotel was César Ritz (1850 – 1918) who went on to found the hotel that bears his name.

Entrance to the Savoy Hotel as seen from the Strand (2008)

---

[36] Source: Official Savoy Group Website

The Savoy enjoyed the patronage of a number of famous guests including Charlie Chaplin and Oscar Wilde. As we have already seen the latter had met Conan Doyle in 1889 at the Langham Hotel. Wilde was also to meet at the Savoy on a number of occasions with Lord Alfred 'Bosie' Douglas and these meetings were an important feature of Wilde's later trial for 'gross indecency'.

Oscar Wilde by Napoleon Sarony (1882)

Sir Arthur Sullivan (1842 – 1900) was on the Savoy board of directors. He is better known as the composing half of Gilbert and Sullivan. Sullivan and the Savoy can both lay claims to connections with Conan Doyle.

Sir Arthur Seymour Sullivan

Around 1892 J.M Barrie put forward the idea for a play to be entitled *Jane Annie*. Initially there were hopes that Sullivan would provide the score but he passed on it and one of his former students took on the project instead. While working on the play Barrie suffered a breakdown and turned to Conan Doyle for help.

Conan Doyle was happy to assist but the resultant play was a flop[37] that closed after a mere fifty performances. The two men however remained friends and Barrie would be present at Conan Doyle's wedding reception when he married Jean Leckie in 1907 (see earlier).

A view of the Cecil and Savoy Hotels from the Thames (early 1900s). The Savoy is on the right

The Savoy's link to Conan Doyle is a lot firmer. Conan Doyle attended a dinner at the hotel on June 18th 1904 that was given in honour of Lord Roberts[38]. Roberts (1832 – 1914) was a Field-Marshal in the British Army and the founding president of the Pilgrims Society, a society that promoted goodwill between Great Britain and the United States.

---

[37] An initial review of the play appeared in the May 15th 1893 issue of the Times.

[38] Source: *On the Trail of Arthur Conan Doyle: An Illustrated Devon Tour* by Brian Pugh and Paul Spiring. The event was reported in the Times (20th June 1904).

Field-Marshal Frederick Sleigh Roberts, 1st Earl Roberts

Roberts fought in the Boer War and it was about this war that Conan Doyle wrote in his book *The Great Boer War* (1900) in which he explained the war as even-handedly as possible in order to contradict a lot of the anti-British sentiment that the war had created. It was this book or rather the earlier pamphlet on which it was based, *The War in South Africa: Its Cause and Conduct*, that Conan Doyle believed earned him his Knighthood in 1902.

Roberts also had the distinction of a brief mention in a Sherlock Holmes story. The adventure entitled *The Blanched Soldier*, which was published in 1926 and set in 1903[39], contains the mention of Roberts' name towards the very end. This was quite apt as the story concerned soldiers who had fought in the Boer War.

The final site of interest on the Strand before it connects with Fleet Street is the church of St. Clement Danes. The building of this church was completed in 1682 by none other than Sir Christopher Wren. On November 24th 1907 a memorial service took place here to mark the death three days previously of Conan Doyle's friend Bertram Fletcher Robinson[40]. This ceremony was held at the same time as Robinson's actual funeral which took place in his home town of Ipplepen, Devon.

---

[39] The date is implied when James Dodd refers to the fact that 1901 was 'just two years ago'.

[40] Source: bfronline.biz.

St. Clement Danes church (2006)

The Lyceum Theatre and William Gillette

In 1772 the Society of Arts founded an exhibition and concert room on the site of the present theatre. However it was not until 1809 that the Lyceum came into its own. The destruction by fire of the nearby Theatre Royal saw its company move to the Lyceum and the Lord Chamberlain granted it the licence it required in order to present plays. The site was rebuilt to the design of architect Samuel Beazley, (1786 – 1851) and opened in 1815. Unfortunately, fifteen years later, the Lyceum suffered the same fate as the Theatre Royal and burned down. Four years later, having been rebuilt, the theatre reopened. Fire struck again seventy years later and the current theatre was built and opened in 1907.

The Lyceum enjoys three links to Conan Doyle and Sherlock Holmes. The first link, chronologically, comes from a visit to London made by Conan Doyle in 1874 when he was fifteen years old[41]. During his stay he visited the Lyceum to watch a performance of Hamlet. It is certainly reasonable to assume that the theatre left a lasting impression as he proceeded to use it for a rendezvous in his second Holmes adventure *The Sign of Four* (1890). In this story Holmes, Watson and Mary Morstan wait for

---

[41] Source: *Conan Doyle: The Man Who Created Sherlock Holmes* by Andrew Lycett. The same events are also mentioned in *The Life of Sir Arthur Conan Doyle* by John Dickson Carr.

contact with Mary's mysterious benefactor at the third pillar from the left outside of the theatre. The story, according to most sources, is set in 1888[42] which means the theatre would have been the one prior to its present incarnation.

The final link is a factual one and concerns Holmes's appearance on stage. In 1901 the American actor William Gillette brought his play *Sherlock Holmes,* which had opened in the United States in 1899, to London. It began with a seven month run at the Lyceum before it went on tour. Its origins lay in the decision by Conan Doyle to sell the rights to the name Sherlock Holmes to Broadway producer Charles Frohman in return for royalties from anything in which it was used[43].

This was followed by Conan Doyle's decision to write a Sherlock Holmes play himself. This was duly sent to Frohman who did not think it good enough to put into production. Frohman travelled to England to tell Conan Doyle this in person and on the same visit suggested that Gillette rewrite it. It is not known to what extent the play was altered as the original manuscript has been lost. It is presumed by some sources that it burned along with Gillette's first draft in the fire that consumed the Baldwin Hotel, San Francisco in 1898 where Gillette was staying while appearing in the play *Secret Service*. Conan Doyle enjoyed top billing on the end result so it could be presumed that some part of his original vision remained intact even if it was substantially rewritten.

---

[42] Once again it is D. Martin Dakin's *A Sherlock Holmes Commentary* and Leslie Klinger's *The New Annotated Sherlock Holmes* that agree on this date.

[43] Source: *Sherlock Holmes – The Published Apocrypha* by Jack Tracy.

William Gillette as Sherlock Holmes

Maude Fealy (1881 – 1971) as Alice Faulkner - Sherlock Holmes's love interest (Courtesy of Roger Johnson)

Madge Larrabee	**Miss Charlotte Granville**
John Forman	**Mr Sydney Herbert**
James Larrabee	**Mr Ralph Delmore**
Terese	**Miss Louise Collins**
Mrs. Faulkner	**Miss Ethel Lorrimore**
Sidney Prince	**Mr Fuller Mellish**
Alice Faulkner	**Miss Maude Fealy**
Sherlock Holmes	**Mr William Gillette**
Professor Moriarty	**Mr W. L. Abingdon**
John	**Mr Soldene Powell**
Alfred Bassick	**Mr Henry Harman**
Billy	**Mr Henry McArdle**
Doctor Watson	**Mr Percy Lyndal**
Jim Craigin	**Mr Griffin Evans**
Thomas Leary	**Mr Henry J. Hadfield**
"Lightfoot" McTague	**Mr Harold Heaton**
Mrs. Smeedley	**Miss Claire Pauncefort**
Parsons	**Mr Frank Pengelly**
Count Von Stalburg	**Mr Walter Selby**
Sir Edward Leighton	**Mr Thomas H. Braidon**

Cast list for original 1901 production taken from 1922 edition of French's Acting Edition[44]

The play was a significant success, attracting such names as the Prince of Wales, and ran for two hundred and sixteen performances before going on tour. Such was the demand by audiences, especially in the United States, that Gillette spent much of the rest of his life giving further performances. Vincent Starrett, author of *The Private Life of Sherlock Holmes*, said that it was 'An absurd, preposterous, and thoroughly delightful melodrama, Mr. Gillette's "Sherlock Holmes" is possibly as

[44] Samuel French Ltd who published this copy of the script had their offices at 26 Southampton Street. This was a relatively short distance from the offices of The Strand Magazine at numbers 8 – 11.

Frederic Dorr Steele has said of it, the best realization of a novelist's conception ever produced upon the stage.'

Lyceum Theatre, Wellington Street (2008)

Sherlock Holmes and the railways

During the course of his adventures Sherlock Holmes and Watson made frequent use of the railways. We have already covered Charing Cross Station but this was by no means the only station mentioned in the stories.

Victoria Station c.1910

Victoria station is the gateway to vast swathes of Kent and the South coast of England. Its principal claim on the Holmes enthusiast is that it is from here that Holmes and Watson catch a train as part of their efforts to elude Professor Moriarty in the adventure *The Final Problem* (1893).

Although it is one large building it was once effectively two stations. The eastern side continues to serve Kent and the western side serves Surrey and Sussex. The western side opened on October 1st 1860[45], was the most impressive and incorporated the Grosvenor Hotel. The eastern half was a considerably less imposing wooden fronted building which opened on August 25th 1862. The dividing wall was removed (in part) in 1924 and the platforms were renumbered from east to west.

Victoria Station in 2008

---

[45] Source: Network Rail.

The station has twice been successfully targeted by terrorists. On the morning of Tuesday February 26th 1884 members of the Irish group called Fenians blew up a station cloakroom[46] and in 1991 the IRA exploded a bomb in a litter bin which killed one person and injured thirty-eight.

Kings Cross Station. The platform shown is number eight. Trains inbound from Cambridge often come into this platform. Holmes and Watson may have arrived at this point on their return from The Missing Three-Quarter (2008)

Kings Cross Station opened on October 14th 1852[47] having been constructed during the previous two years. When it opened it had

---

[46] This event and the efforts to clean up the damage were reported in the Times issued Thursday 28th February 1884.

[47] *The Face of London.*

eight platforms but only numbers one and eight were used, the others were used purely as sidings. It is rumoured that platform eight covers the burial site of Queen Boudicca[48], the Queen of the Iceni tribe and the scourge of the Roman Empire.

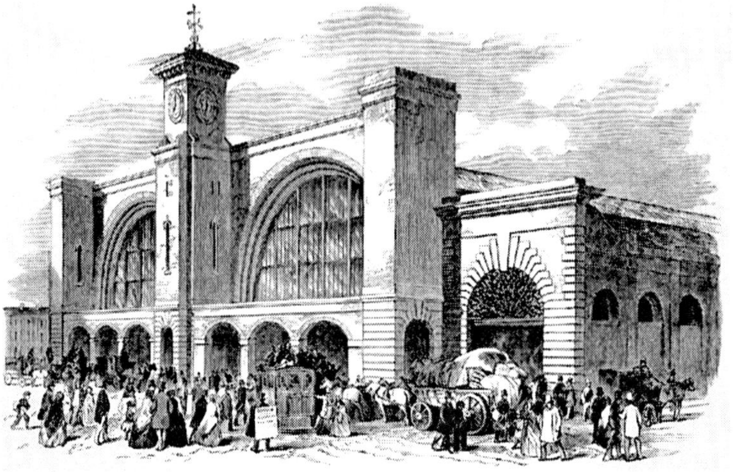

Drawing of Kings Cross Station soon after its opening in 1852

The station was designed by Lewis Cubitt (1799 - 1883) who, with his elder brother Thomas (1788 - 1855), made a significant contribution to London architecture[49]. Thomas was a leading Master Builder in London and was responsible for building several sites designed by his brother Lewis.

---

[48] Source: Network Rail Website.

[49] There was also another brother called William (1791 - 1863). He had less interest in architecture but was interested in engineering and politics. Towards the end of his life he served two terms as Lord Mayor of London.

The father of the Cubitt brothers was a Norfolk farmer and it is therefore apt that Cubitt was responsible for the design of a station that runs trains into West Norfolk[50]. The Cubitt name is common in Norfolk and features in the Sherlock Holmes adventure *The Dancing Men*. However Conan Doyle's decision to make Holmes's client a Cubitt has nothing to with this Cubitt family. In fact he named the character after the Cubitt family that ran the Hill House Public House in which he often stayed during his visits to Norfolk[51].

The link for the Holmes fan lies in the fact that it is from Kings Cross Station that Holmes and Watson travel to Cambridge in their search for Godfrey Staunton in *The Missing Three-Quarter.*

Paddington Station is one of the most mentioned in the Sherlock Holmes Canon. Holmes and Watson catch trains from Paddington to places outside of London in three stories – *The Boscombe Valley Mystery, Silver Blaze* and *The Hound of the Baskervilles*. Watson and his wife Mary lived near to Paddington Station in the immediate aftermath of their marriage and his link with the station was the means by which the adventure known as *The Engineer's Thumb* was brought to Holmes's notice.

The station was opened in 1838 but the current building dates from 1854 and was designed by Isambard Kingdom Brunel. Nine years later the first underground rail line was opened between

---

[50] The routes that travel through Cambridge often end in Kings Lynn.

[51] More on this can be found in the later section on Liverpool Street Station.

Paddington and Farringdon and this was to become what is known today as the Metropolitan Line.

Train in Paddington Station 1914

Victor Hatherley shows Doctor Watson his injury in his Paddington consulting room.

As we have come to expect, where there is a station there is a hotel. In this case we have the Great Western Hotel. This hotel was designed by Philip Charles Hardwick, the son of Philip Hardwick (see later) and built by the Cubitts who, as we have seen, were responsible for the building of Kings Cross Station. The hotel, now trading under the name Hilton London Paddington, was built between 1851 and 1854 and from the late nineteenth century until 1983 was run directly by the railway company.

The Great Western Hotel c1854 from The Illustrated London News

The Paddington area itself contains a number of interesting connections. One of its most infamous sons (although he was not so at the time) was John Charles Netley.

John Charles Netley

Netley (1860 – 1903) was a cabbie and tragically died when he was thrown from his own cab, trampled by his horses and had his head crushed by the vehicle wheels. In 1976 this little known man became famous when the Jack the Ripper 'Royal Conspiracy Theory' gained widespread attention courtesy of the author Stephen Knight. The theory alleges that this same John Netley drove the royal surgeon Sir William Gull (see later) around Whitechapel in a coach thus acting not only as an accessory to the murders but also as the means of the killer's many escapes from justice.

The area can also lay claim to events connected with St Mary's Hospital. This hospital, through which Watson could have gained work directly or indirectly, was founded in 1845 and had its own medical school. Sir Alexander Fleming (1881 – 1955) discovered Penicillin in the hospital's laboratory and Sir

Bernard Spilsbury (1877 – 1947), who occasionally conducted research in the same laboratory, was a pioneering British pathologist whose evidence helped to convict many murderers including Dr Crippen.

Dr Crippen

St Mary's Hospital (2008)

Euston Station c1900

Euston station, opened in 1837, was designed by Philip Hardwick (1792 – 1870). It features in three Sherlock Holmes adventures – *A Study in Scarlet*, *The Priory School* and *The Blanched Soldier*. The station had the distinction of being the first inter-city station built in London and, during the time of Holmes and Conan Doyle, it was owned by the London and North Western Railway. Today it is owned by Network Rail.

During the 1840s the station was improved and extended. One of the principal additions was the great hall which was designed by Hardwick's son[52] and opened on May 27th 1849.

---

[52] This would not be the only time that the son succeeded the father. They also both held the same position at St. Bartholomew's Hospital (see later).

The Great Hall at Euston Station from around the time it opened in 1849

In *A Study in Scarlet* it is from Euston that Drebber and Stangerson plan to take a train to Liverpool before their plans are upset by events. In *The Priory School* it is from Euston that Holmes and Watson accompany Dr Huxtable to Mackleton, where the school of the title is situated[53], so that they can investigate the disappearance of Lord Saltire. Finally, it is in *The*

---

[53] Mackleton does not exist as a place but we can surmise where Conan Doyle got the name from. The school is described as being in the 'Peak country'. This, of course, means the Peak District which covers land in several counties. One of these counties is Cheshire and, according to the 1891 census, people of the name Mackleton only lived in that county. It could just be a coincidence but, if so, a remarkable one.

Blanched Soldier that Holmes, James Dodd and Sir James Saunders travel to Bedfordshire from Euston to investigate the strange behaviour of the Emsworth family.

Sadly in the 1960s, in what can only be described as an act of historical and architectural vandalism, the station building and arch were demolished[54] to make way for a new station which opened in 1968. This station is now the home for Network Rail.

Euston Station (2004)

Finally, Euston station was also the site of the start of a business which still exists today. W H Smith opened their first book stall at Euston Station on November 1st 1848[55].

---

[54] According to *The Face of London* the hope was that the arch would be re-erected in the station gardens. Alas this was not to be.

[55] *The Face of London.*

Waterloo station opened in the same year and was one of the most regularly used stations by Holmes, Watson and their clients. The station is explicitly referred to in six stories.

Waterloo Station main entrance (2008) Photograph by Sunil060902

The station was originally owned by the London and South Western Railway and was initially called Waterloo Bridge Station after the bridge which was close by. It only adopted its current name in 1886. At the time it opened it had only three platforms and a maximum service of fourteen trains a day[56].

---

[56] *The Face of London.* By the time Clunn wrote his book the station had increased in size and accommodated twenty-one platforms and a normal service of one thousand two hundred trains a day.

As remarked above, this was a significant station in no less than six stories. The first of these was *The Five Orange Pips* where the unfortunate John Openshaw's body is fished out of the Thames by Waterloo Bridge after his visit to Holmes. This is one of the few cases where Holmes's client is murdered before the solution to the case is determined and one of the few cases where Holmes comes close to taking events personally.

John Openshaw arrives at Baker Street, from Waterloo, to see Holmes shortly before his death (as drawn by Sidney Paget)

The second of the stories to concern the station was *The Speckled Band.* It is this story, as already mentioned, that enjoys the distinction of being Conan Doyle's favourite of all the Holmes adventures. Helen Stoner arrives at Waterloo from Stoke Moran en route to consult Holmes regarding the events surrounding the strange death of her sister Julia.

The station is also the point of departure for Holmes and Watson when they head to Aldershot to investigate the death of Colonel Barclay as told in *The Crooked Man.* It is used again to head to Woking in *The Naval Treaty* and to head to Farnham in Surrey during *The Solitary Cyclist.*

Victoria Embankment c1900 - Waterloo Bridge, the site of John Openshaw's murder, can be seen in the distance

The most famous story to contain references to this station is *The Hound of the Baskervilles*. This story was published before *The Solitary Cyclist* but after all the others stories involving the station. It is not only the station at which Dr Mortimer and Baskerville meet but it is also the station to which Stapleton flees after his tailing of Baskerville is discovered by Holmes. This in itself provides an interesting line of enquiry. Earlier, in our look at the Northumberland Avenue hotels, we examined the conversation between Holmes and the cabman John Clayton. Clayton mentions in this conversation that he was ordered suddenly to get from Regent Street to Waterloo Station. This course of action, as we know, was triggered by Stapleton realising that he had been spotted. Clayton reports that Stapleton then disappeared into the station presumably to catch a train back to Dartmoor.

Train leaving Waterloo Station c1904

This does not make sense. We know from the end of the story that Stapleton had brought his wife up to London with him and had imprisoned her at the hotel in which they had been staying. Therefore if he had fled to Waterloo and boarded a train he would have left his wife in London. This is clearly unlikely. So we are left with only two possibilities. The first is that Stapleton had sent his wife to the station to either wait for him or travel ahead of him. This is highly unlikely as the whole reason he had brought her to London in the first place was the fact that he did not trust her after her refusal to assist him in bringing about the death of Sir Charles Baskerville. Therefore he was unlikely to leave her free and to her own devices.

The only remaining possibility therefore is that after Clayton had left him at Waterloo Stapleton must have caught another cab all the way back to his hotel in order to collect his imprisoned wife and return via Waterloo back to Dartmoor. It is not a satisfying answer as it is decidedly impractical but it is the only theory that fits the events as described.

Liverpool Street Station 1896

Liverpool Street Station opened in 1874 and was fully operational in 1875. The station was designed by Edward Wilson[57] and built on the site of the first Bethlem Royal Hospital otherwise known as Bedlam. The former Great Eastern Hotel which adjoins the station was designed by E. M. Barry who was also responsible for the hotels at Charing Cross station and Cannon Street station (see later). The station was named after the street which in turn was named after the former Prime Minister Lord Liverpool (1770 – 1828).

---

[57] Born 1821, date of death unknown.

Conan Doyle and his friend Bertram Fletcher Robinson enjoyed a golfing holiday in Cromer during 1901[58]. It is highly probable that they travelled from Liverpool Street as this is the only station from which you can reach Cromer directly[59]. Robinson and Conan Doyle had, during a trip between South Africa and England in 1901, discussed legends of phantom hounds but it was a resumption of this discussion while in Cromer that eventually led to them agreeing to work on a story together[60]. The proposed joint project did not materialise[61] but

---

[58] Source: *On the Trail of Arthur Conan Doyle: An Illustrated Devon Tour* by Brian Pugh and Paul Spiring.

[59] The argument for the journey being made by train is also strengthened by the fact that Conan Doyle is not known to have bought a car until 1903. According to authors Brian Pugh and Paul Spiring, Fletcher Robinson wrote articles about motor racing for *Pearson's Magazine* in 1902 and 1903 and therefore may well have been able to drive but he was not in possession of a car at the time of his death.

[60] Source: *On the Trail of Arthur Conan Doyle: An Illustrated Devon Tour* by Brian Pugh and Paul Spiring.

[61] The decision by Conan Doyle to use Sherlock Holmes in the story was probably one of the reasons that the collaboration with Fletcher Robinson did not happen in quite the same way as the two men had originally conceived. At some point after this he must have decided against the idea of collaborating with anyone in the future. In 1911 a man named Arthur Whitaker sent him a Sherlock Holmes pastiche entitled *The Man who was Wanted* and suggested that they collaborate. Conan Doyle refused citing the reason that if he were to collaborate with anyone it would drive down the price he could get from editors. He offered to buy Whitaker's idea for ten guineas claiming, in his letter, that he had done this once before (paying the same amount). This

Conan Doyle went on to use the idea as the basis for his most famous Sherlock Holmes story *The Hound of the Baskervilles*. More details on Conan Doyle's friendship with Robinson and how the story was conceived can be found in *Bertram Fletcher Robinson: A Footnote to The Hound of the Baskervilles* by Brian Pugh and Paul Spiring.

As mentioned earlier, Conan Doyle enjoyed a number of holidays in Norfolk and it was on one such holiday in 1903 that he penned the adventure *The Dancing Men*. In this he named Holmes's client Hilton Cubitt. As we have already seen the Cubitt name is common in Norfolk and Conan Doyle borrowed the name from his hosts. In the story Hilton Cubitt travels from North Walsham in Norfolk to London arriving at Liverpool Street Station before heading to Baker Street. Naturally it is also from here that Holmes and Watson travel to Cubitt's house to ultimately aid in the capture of Cubitt's killer Abe Slaney.

---

however cannot be accurate. We know from *On the Trail of Arthur Conan Doyle* (see above footnote) that Conan Doyle bought the idea for creating a fake thumbprint with a wax impression from Fletcher Robinson. However this idea, which was used in *The Norwood Builder*, was purchased for fifty pounds not ten guineas. We also know from *Bertram Fletcher Robinson: A Footnote to the Hound of the Baskervilles* that Conan Doyle had paid Robinson five hundred pounds in 1901 for his contribution to *The Hound of the Baskervilles*. Therefore he was being at the least misleading to Whitaker in his letter. Perhaps Whitaker was encouraged to approach Conan Doyle in the first place having been aware of Robinson's involvement in *The Hound of the Baskervilles*.

Lord Liverpool, Prime Minister between 1812 and 1827, after whom Liverpool Street and, by extension, the station are named.

The next station of interest is Cannon Street Station which opened on September 1st 1866. It was designed by Sir John Hawkshaw (the designer of Charing Cross Station) and his pupil John Wolfe-Barry[62] (1836 – 1918).

John Wolfe-Barry co-designer of Cannon Street Station

It is from this station that Neville St. Clair caught his train home to Lee from the City after plying his trade as the beggar Hugh Boone in *The Man with the Twisted Lip*. Holmes, when explaining the background of the case to Watson, states that St. Clair always took the 5.14pm train from Cannon Street back to Lee each evening.

---

[62] On January 22nd 1901 the now knighted Sir John instigated the first meeting of the Council of the Institution of Civil Engineers. This body was set up with the aim of standardising the size of iron and steel sections used in construction. This eventually led to the creation of the British Standards Institution in 1929. The British Standard Mark, otherwise known as the Kitemark® came into being in 1903.

Illustration of the Cannon Street Hotel c1910

In 1867 a hotel was added to the station at a cost of £100,000[63] (see above picture). This was designed by E. M. Barry who, as we have already mentioned, designed the hotel in front of Charing Cross Station. In many respects the design was very similar right down to the forecourt in front of the hotel. Presumably because of its position in relation to the city, the function rooms were greatly in demand by local businesses for meetings and even when the hotel closed the rooms were still hired out by the building's owners for the use of financial institutions and other businesses.

---

[63] *The Face of London* by Harold P. Clunn.

Illustration of Cannon Street Station as it was c1910

Cannon Street (2005)

The final station of interest is London Bridge. This station opened in December 1836 and was for many years the most important station in the south of London[64]. This importance stemmed primarily from its role as the destination station for City workers. In 1853 the station was expanded[65] in anticipation of the extra traffic that would need to get to and from the relocated and soon to be opened Crystal Palace (see later).

In 1861 the London Bridge Terminus Hotel opened but it was destined to be a very short lived hotel. A mere thirty-one years later it was turned into offices for the railway company and was finally demolished in 1941[66]. Sir John Hawkshaw, who as we have seen designed Charing Cross Station, also had a hand in the design of London Bridge. The roof that covered the newly extended station in 1866 was designed by Hawkshaw along with a F. D. Banister.

It was to this station that Jonas Oldacre came from Norwood en route to visit John Hector McFarlane in *The Norwood Builder* (see later). It was also at this station that Watson spotted Holmes's rival Barker on his way back from Blackheath in *The Retired Colourman.*

---

[64] It was also the first London Station and was originally two stations. It is for this reason that the station has some terminal platforms as well as some that go through to Charing Cross, Cannon Street and other destinations.

[65] *The Face of London* by Harold P. Clunn.

[66] Network Rail.

From the mid 1800s right up to the 1960s the standard reference for train times was *Bradshaw's Monthly Railway Guide* known as the *Bradshaw* for short.

George Bradshaw creator of the Bradshaw Railway Timetable (1841)

The timetable was created by George Bradshaw (1801 – 1853) a cartographer, printer and publisher. He was already well known having published books mapping the canals of Lancashire and Yorkshire. In 1839 the first collection of railway timetables was published entitled *Bradshaw's Railway Time Tables and Assistant to Railway Travelling.*

In 1841 the timetable began to be published monthly and was a mere eight pages long. Fifty-seven years later it would reach nearly a thousand. So popular were the timetables that Bradshaw's name became synonymous with timetables even when they had been produced by someone else.

YORK, SCARBOROUGH, PICKERING, & WHITBY—York and North Midland.

Miles	Fares from N'castle & Darlington to York, pp 70 & 71; from Leeds & Normanton to York, page 77.	Down. 1*2 gov.	1 2 3 mrn	1 2 3 noon	1 2 3 aft	Sundays 1*2 morn	Fares 1st s. d.	2nd s. d.	3rd s. d.
—	**York**........dep.	7 0	..	12 0	5 30	7+0	..	..	..
4½	Haxby	7 7	..	12 7	5 37	7 7	1 0	0 9	0 6
6¾	Strensall	7 12	..	12 12	5 42	7 12	1 6	1 0	0 9
9¾	Flaxton	7 20	..	12 19	5 48	7 20	2 0	1 6	1 0
11¾	Barton	7 25	..	12 25	5 55	7 25	2 6	2 0	1 6
15¼	Kirkham	7 35	..	12 35	6 5	7 35	3 6	2 6	2 0
16	Castle Howard......	7 39	..	12 39	6 9	7 39	3 6	2 6	2 0
18½	Hutton	7 45	..	12 45	6 15	7 45	4 0	3 0	2 3
21½	**Malton**	8 0	..	1 0	6 30	8 0	5 0	3 6	2 6
25¾	Rillington, Whitby J.	8 10	..	1 10	6 40	8 10	6 0	4 0	3 0
Whitby Branch.	— Rillingtn. for Wby.	8 10	10 3	1 20	6 40	8 0	..	..	..
29¼	Marishes Road ..	8 20	10 13	1 30	6 45	8 10	..	..	..
32¼	**Pickering**	8 35	10 30	1 40	7 0	8 30	8 0	5 6	4 0
38¼	Levisham	8 45	..	2 15	7 15	8 45	..	..	..
47¼	Goathland	9 15	..	2 50	7 45	9 15	..	..	..
50¼	Grosmont	9 40	..	3 10	8 0	9 40	..	..	..
53½	Sleights.........	9 50	..	3 32	8 22	9 50	..	..	..
54¾	Ruswarp	9 55	..	3 40	8 25	9 55	..	..	..
56¼	**Whitby** ....arr.	10 0	..	3 45	8 30	10 0	12 0	9 6	7 0
37¾	Knapton	8 19	..	1 19	6 49	8 19	6 6	4 6	3 0
39¼	Heslerton	8 23	..	1 25	6 53	8 23	6 6	4 6	3 6
33	Sherburn	8 32	..	1 32	7 2	8 32	7 6	5 6	4 0
34½	Ganton	8 36	..	1 36	7 6	8 36	8 0	5 6	4 0
38½	Seamer	8 44	..	1 44	7 9	8 44	9 0	6 6	4 6
44½	Filey	9 25	..	2 25	..	..	10 6	7 6	5 6
42½	**Scarborough** arr	9 0	..	2 0	7 30	9 0	10 0	7 0	5 0

Miles	Stations.	Up. 1 2 3 mrn	1+2 morn	1 2 3 aft	1 2 3 aft	Sundays 1 2 3 mrn	1*+2 aft
—	**Scarborough**....dep	..	9 30	12 15	4* 5	..	4 5
9	Filey................	..	..	10 56	3 51	..	..
3½	Seamer	..	9 44	12 25	4 15	..	4 15
7¾	Ganton...............	..	9 52	12 36	4 26	..	4 26
9¼	Sherburn.............	..	9 56	12 40	4 35	..	4 35
12¾	Heslerton............	..	10 5	12 48	4 38	..	4 38
14½	Knapton	..	10 9	12 52	4 40	..	4 41
16½	Rillington, Whitby Junc	..	10 18	1 0	4 50	..	4 50
Whitby Branch. 47	**Whitby** ......dep.	..	8 15	..	3 0	..	3 0
45½	Ruswarp.............	..	8 20	..	3 5	..	3 5
44	Sleights	..	8 25	..	3 10	..	3 10
41	Grosmont	..	8 35	..	3 20	..	3 20
38	Goathland	..	8 50	..	3 40	..	3 40
29	Levisham	..	9 25	..	4 5	..	4 5
23	**Pickering**........	7 20	9 45	12 20	4 25	7 20	4 25
20	Marishes Road......	7 30	9 55	12 35	4 35	7 30	4 35
16½	Rillington	7 50	10 5	12 50	4 50	7 40	4 50
21	**Malton**............	..	10 30	1 10	5 0	..	5 0
23½	Hutton...............	..	10 38	1 20	5 7	..	5 7
26½	Castle Howard	..	10 45	1 25	5 12	..	5 12
27	Kirkham.............	..	10 48	1 30	5 15	..	5 15
30½	Barton	..	10 58	1 40	5 26	..	5 25
32½	Flaxton..............	..	11 4	1 45	5 30	..	5 30
35½	Strensall............	..	11 10	1 50	5 38	..	5 38
37½	Haxby...............	..	11 15	1 56	5 43	..	5 43
42½	**York**..............arr	..	11 30	2 10	6 0	..	6 0

An omnibus for Castle Howard meets the trains at Castle Howard Station. Every York fortnightly fair a special train will leave Malton at 6 morn.
York to Thirsk, Darlington, & Newcastle, page 68.
To Leeds, Normanton, Wakefield, Halifax, and Manchester, pages 77 and 78. * Mail trains. † Gov. trains.

Example of a Bradshaw listing from 1850

The last official Bradshaw guide was published in 1961 over one hundred years after its founder's death in 1853. Bradshaw died in Norway from cholera and was buried in Oslo. The guide is referenced in two Sherlock Holmes adventures. In *The Copper Beeches* Holmes instructs Watson to look up the trains from London and Watson discovers the 9.30am from Waterloo which arrives in Winchester at 11.30[67]. The second reference to the Bradshaw guide comes from *The Valley of Fear* when Holmes and Watson briefly consider it the book required to decipher the code sent to them by Porlock – Holmes's informer from inside Professor Moriarty's organisation.

---

[67] The journey is somewhat faster today and the nearest comparable train leaves Waterloo at 9.35am arriving at 10.32am.

British Museum and Museum Tavern

British Museum 1903

The British Museum opened to the public in 1759 having been established six years earlier. At the time the museum was based at Montague House and it remained there until the 1840s when the building was demolished to make room for the present museum.

The museum was initially based on the royal library of King George II and the natural history collection of Sir Hans Sloane (1660 – 1753) who bequeathed his collection to the nation. Sloane was a man of many talents who was not only an expert in natural history but also a physician, admitted as a fellow to the Royal College of Physicians in 1687. He was also a member of the Royal Society. Some years later he achieved the distinction of becoming president of both organisations. In the latter case succeeding Sir Isaac Newton.

Sir Hans Sloane

The Holmes and Conan Doyle connections to the museum and area are considerable. Conan Doyle was a user of the library and was an occasional customer of the Museum Tavern across the street (see later). For a brief time he also lived very close to the museum at 23 Montague Place. This is one of the four streets that border the museum and runs along the northern side. We know of Conan Doyle's residence from the 1891 census where his profession was listed as ophthalmic surgeon. As we have already seen he travelled daily from this location to his practice at Upper Wimpole Street. An interesting error appears on the census where Conan Doyle's wife is listed as being of the same profession as her husband. The error was corrected but it is still interesting to see it there.

Turning to the Holmes connections, clearly Conan Doyle retained some fondness for the area as a number of stories refer to both the museum and surrounding streets. Conan Doyle's old address of Montague Place is given as the address of Violet Hunter when she writes to Holmes seeking his aid in *The Copper Beeches*. Regrettably Conan Doyle did not give the exact number of the house at which Miss Hunter stayed but it is tempting to think that he had his old address in mind when he wrote the story. His decision to use the street as her address may well have been connected to the fact that he had only moved away from the area to South Norwood about a year prior to its publication.

The museum is mentioned in several of the Holmes adventures. In *The Red Circle* Mrs Warren's boarding house is described as being located to the north-east of the museum buildings and, in *Wisteria Lodge,* Holmes visits the museum to read up on Voodoo practices. He visits it again in *The Hound of the Baskervilles* when he goes to find more information on the villain Stapleton. Finally in the adventure *The Blue Carbuncle* Henry Baker works at the museum and is an occasional visitor to the nearby Alpha Inn (see later).

The final and arguably most important connection is that one of the other streets bordering the museum is Montague Street. This road is very important to the Holmes enthusiast as it marks the location of Holmes's first known lodgings upon his arrival in London. We first learn this in *The Musgrave Ritual* when Holmes describes the case to Watson.

Montague House, seen roughly in the centre of this drawing of 1828, as it was when it held the British Museum collection. The new building is being constructed to the right.

The Museum Tavern was known in the early eighteenth century as The Dog and Duck. This was due to the fact that it wanted to be associated with the hunting that took place in the vicinity. John Creed became landlord in 1762[68] and renamed the tavern to its present name in an effort to link it with the British Museum which had been established nine years earlier.

The Museum Tavern (2007)

According to the magazine *Time Out* Conan Doyle was an occasional customer here. Presumably he visited on his return from his ophthalmic practice to his home in Montague Place or after visiting the museum itself.

---

[68] Source: Campaign for Real Ale (North London Website).

In 1855 the tavern was extended by the architect William Finch Hill and a lot of what you see in the tavern today dates from that extension although there were more alterations in 1889 by the architects Wylson & Long.

The Museum Tavern is a good candidate for the Alpha Inn from *The Blue Carbuncle*[69]. Henry Baker, in whose goose the gem is found, describes to Holmes and Watson how he bought the goose from the landlord of the Alpha and further describes it as being near the museum. Given the large number of public houses in the vicinity of the museum this is not much help in locating the real place that Conan Doyle had in mind. The fact that he allegedly drank there does however lend weight to its candidature.

However there is an alternative candidate. When Holmes and Watson visit the Alpha it is described as 'a small public-house at the corner of one of the streets which runs down into Holborn'. This certainly fits the description of the Museum Tavern (which still remains the best candidate) but it could also be a reasonable description of another pub called The Plough located on Museum Street.

---

[69] This is according to Charles Viney in his book *Sherlock Holmes in London*.

The Plough (2008)

Holborn

Holborn is only a few minutes walk from Oxford Street and the British Museum and the name applies to the district and its principal street. It is derived from 'Old Bourne' which means 'Old Brook'. It is one of the few areas of London to have escaped the Great Fire and in the nineteenth century it was quite an entertainment centre with over twenty inns and taverns recorded in the 1860s.

High Holborn c1910

Despite this the inns, taverns and shops were generally of a lower quality. This was because Holborn occupied something of a no mans land in London. The area was too far west to be of interest to the workers in the City but at the same time it was too far to the east for the wealthy residents of the West End[70].

The connection to the Holmes stories lies in the fact that a restaurant called The Holborn once stood in this street at the point where it joins with Kingsway. It was sadly demolished in the 1950s[71] but it was to this location that Dr Watson brought his former colleague Stamford after their meeting at the Criterion (see earlier). The legendary meeting with Holmes at St Bartholomew's Hospital would have been a short drive east eventually arriving in King Edward Street from where the hospital could be accessed.

Drawing of High Holborn in the opposite direction c1900

---

[70] Source: *A Dictionary of Victorian London* by Lee Jackson.

[71] Source: *Sherlock Holmes in London* by Charles Viney.

Woodcut of The Holborn restaurant

Conan Doyle himself visited this same restaurant on May 31st 1892 for the annual dinner of the Incorporated Society of Authors[72]. Among the many guests was H. Rider Haggard – the author of *King Solomon's Mines*. This dinner was some time after the publication of *A Study in Scarlet* so it is tempting to wonder whether his decision to use the restaurant in that story was inspired by an earlier visit. He may also have visited it during his residence in Montague Place which is only about five to ten minutes walk away.

---

[72] This dinner was reported in the June 1st 1892 issue of the Times.

Tottenham Court Road

Tottenham Court Road is well known as being the street to visit for people requiring electronic equipment. In fact in this regard it is as identified with electronics as Harley Street is with medicine. It runs from St Giles' Circus[73] northwards where it ultimately connects with Euston Road.

Tottenham Court Road c1930. In Holmes's time the Dominion Theatre did not exist. The site was occupied by Meux's Brewery.

---

[73] St Giles' Circus is the junction of Oxford Street and Charing Cross Road.

The southern end of the road (as shown in the above photograph) is very close to the British Museum and thus very close to Montague Place. Conan Doyle would have very likely crossed this road when walking between his home and his ophthalmic practice in Upper Wimpole Street. It is also possible that his route provided useful information for use in later stories.

Thanks to the myriad number of intersecting streets between Montague Place and Upper Wimpole Street there were a large number of possible routes for Conan Doyle to walk in order to reach his practice. As he was somewhat lacking in patients he may well have made the journey at a leisurely pace and varied his route. It is interesting to note that one road that connects with Regent Street, which he could have easily travelled, is called Mortimer Street. It is highly tempting to speculate that it was this road that provided the name for Dr Mortimer from *The Hound of the Baskervilles*.

It is also possible that another of the streets in the area provided a name for a character. Of the four adventures that explicitly mention Tottenham Court Road the latest was *The Red Circle* which was published in 1911 as part of the series known as *His Last Bow*. This story featured a Mr and Mrs Warren. The former works as a timekeeper in Tottenham Court Road and the latter, who becomes Holmes's client, runs a boarding house a short distance from the British Museum on Great Orme Street[74].

---

[74] This street does not exist and the name is therefore likely to be a cover for an existing street. Great Orme Street is described as being on the north-eastern side of the museum but the proximity to the museum is unclear. The street immediately to the north-east is Montague Street but this is unlikely to be the street in question as Conan Doyle had already named it explicitly in *The Musgrave Ritual* as the site of Holmes's first London lodgings. The street that runs parallel to this

At the northern end of Tottenham Court Road, just before it connects to Euston Road there is a Warren Street which runs parallel to Euston Road until it connects with Cleveland Street. Could this street have lent its name to the couple? Even if it did not it is still an interesting coincidence.

Prior to *The Red Circle* there were three other stories with a connection to Tottenham Court Road. The road was the site of the plumbing business of Mary Sutherland's late father as described in *A Case of Identity*. The junction of Tottenham Court Road with Goodge Street was the scene of the scuffle between Mr Henry Baker and the 'roughs' that resulted in the former losing his Christmas Goose in *The Blue Carbuncle*. Finally in *The Cardboard Box* we learn that Holmes bought his Stradivarius violin from a 'Jew broker's' on this very road.

---

street is Bedford Place but this does not quite fit the description from the story. Further north-east brings you into the streets surrounding Great Ormond Street Hospital. The similarity of the street names is naturally interesting but the road is described as a 'narrow thoroughfare' which is hardly descriptive of Great Ormond Street.

Covent Garden

Covent Garden is well known as the location of the Royal Opera House and Covent Garden Market and it is a location that is bordered by several areas that have already been covered. To the north-east is High Holborn, to the north-west is Soho, to the south is the Strand and to the south-west is St James's where Pall Mall is located.

Drawing of Covent Garden Market 1902

The market today sells clothes, flowers and a considerable number of souvenirs for the tourists that flock to the area. However it was not always as it is now. From the 1500s to 1974 the market was largely dedicated to fruit and vegetables. It was only when the increased modern traffic coming to and from the market threatened to bring the West End to a standstill that the fruit and vegetable market was relocated and replaced with the current offering.

It was in the early 17th century that the area started to look much as it does today. The design was carried out by Inigo Jones (1573 – 1652) who, amongst other projects, was also responsible for the modernisation of Whitehall. The area soon became a site for market traders and, following the Great Fire, it became even more important as the sites of many neighbouring markets had been destroyed. It was here that the first recorded performance of an English Punch and Judy show took place[75] and the pub that faces onto the west piazza goes by that name today.

Holmes examines the books of Mr. Breckinridge at Covent Garden Market in The Blue Carbuncle

[75] This occurred in 1662 according the diarist Samuel Pepys.

The principal Holmes connection lies in the story *The Blue Carbuncle*. It is from the Covent Garden market that the landlord of the Alpha Inn purchased the geese which formed his goose club. One of these geese briefly ends up in the hands of Henry Baker before his encounter in Tottenham Court Road (see earlier). Subsequently Holmes and Watson visit the stall of the vendor Mr Breckinridge and, via a wager, secure details about where the geese were purchased from.

Conan Doyle himself can also claim a connection to this famous location. On July 9th 1919 he decided to comment on the running of the market. He wrote a letter to the Times, entitled *Profiteering – Where the Guilt Lies*, in which he denounced retailers of food throughout the country. In particular he focused on Covent Garden, as he had first-hand experience, and accused its stall holders of profiteering at the expense of both the growers and the market's customers. The price of cabbages and lettuces in particular came in for strong criticism and he went so far as to suggest that such prices, if left unchecked, would lead to 'violence in this country'. He then suggested that legislation should be put in place to prevent what he clearly saw as a most offensive practice. His comments soon drew an aggressive response. On July 11th 1919 a number of people including F. R. Ridley, President of the London Fruit, Flower and Vegetable Market Association, put their names to a letter[76] in which Conan Doyle was taken to task for his 'unwarrantable attack' and challenged to back up his claims. The letter further stated that it was wrong for a man 'who has the ear of the public' to make such unfounded claims as it could severely damage the livelihoods of all parties connected to the market.

---

[76] This letter was printed in the Times of the same date.

This was by no means the only letter on the subject. A Mr W.B. Shearn, a fruiterer on Tottenham Court Road, actually offered to donate ten pounds to a charity of Conan Doyle's choice if he could back up his claim by indicating even one retailer who was profiteering. He also questioned the effect that Conan Doyle's word could have on the public at large. It is not known whether the gauntlet was picked up but if it was there was no further mention of it in the Times.

However not everyone was aghast at Conan Doyle's letter. On July 12th 1919 a farmer, who chose to go under the anonymous name of 'Market Gardener' wrote in support of Conan Doyle's stance and even extended the claim stating that almost all retailers were profiteering at the expense of suppliers.

Inigo Jones, designer of Covent Garden, as painted by Hogarth based on an earlier painting by Van Dyck

St Bartholomew's Hospital

The Square of St Bartholomew's Hospital c1920

St Bartholomew's Hospital or Bart's as it is more commonly known was founded in 1123 and is the oldest hospital in England. The main square, shown above, was designed by the architect James Gibbs (1682 – 1754) although not everything you see in the photograph above was there from the start. The fountain that can be seen in the centre of the square was installed in 1859 and on the outer wall, quite close to the King Henry VIII gate, is a plaque dedicated to William Wallace (of Braveheart fame) who was executed just outside.

The official surveyor to the hospital was Philip Hardwick who, as we have already mentioned, designed Euston Station.

Hardwick had effectively inherited from this position from his father and was later to pass the role on to his own son.

The King Henry VIII Gate – This is still the main entrance to the hospital (2007)

As the dedicated fan will know, it is here that the first meeting occurs between Watson and Holmes. The meeting takes place in one of the hospital laboratories and was illustrated quite effectively by the artist George Hutchinson.

Stamford introduces Watson to Sherlock Holmes in this drawing by George Hutchinson

According to at least three sources, this event (and the subsequent events of *A Study in Scarlet*) occurred in 1881[77]. The

---

[77] W.S Baring-Gould, Dakin and Klinger all agree on this date.

story itself was published in 1887. These two years are significant as they coincide with two important events in the history of Bart's and perhaps British medical care as a whole.

In 1881, in which the events of the story are set, Ethel Gordon Manson (1856/7 - 1947) became the first Matron of the hospital (at the age of 24). This was quite an achievement as medicine was still something of a closed shop to women. Despite opposition she instituted a great many improvements in patient care, fought for the proper recognition of the nursing profession and set the standard for nursing for the future. Her achievements did not end there however. She set the standard for the nursing uniform and brought in the different colours and patterns that denoted the different grades of nursing. In addition she founded the *British Journal of Nursing,* which still exists today, and was the first President of the International Council of Nurses (founded in July 1899) a position she held for five years.

In 1887, the year the story was published, Manson married a doctor called Bedford-Fenwick and was forced to resign her post. This was down to the belief at the time that it was improper for a married woman to be a hospital matron. However this did not mark the end of her medical career and in the very same year she resigned her post the first student nurses entered the hospital.

It is also interesting to note that for a time she lived at number 20 Upper Wimpole Street, near to the site of Conan Doyle's former ophthalmic practice, and this site was commemorated with an English Heritage plaque in 1999[78].

---

[78] Source: English Heritage Website

Brook Street

Brook Street (2006) looking from east to west

Brook Street[79] is the scene of one of Holmes's best displays of deduction. It is at number 403 during the adventure *The Resident Patient* that Holmes deduces all of the events leading to the death of the unfortunate Mr Blessington from an examination of the

[79] The name is derived from Tyburn Brook.

various items of evidence found in his bedroom where he had been discovered hanging.

Holmes examines a cigar in the room of the late Mr Blessington in The Resident Patient (1893)

As has been reported in other works, Brook Street does not have a number 403 and this is yet another example of Conan Doyle hiding the true location he had in mind (if indeed he had one at all). In addition to its Sherlockian connection, the road does have another albeit tenuous link to Victorian Crime.

Number 74 Brook Street was home for a while to Sir William Gull (1816 – 1890) and was the location where he died as a result of a series of strokes. Gull had enjoyed a distinguished medical career and was created a Baronet in 1872 in recognition of the medical care he provided to the Royal Family. As we have already mentioned, in our look at Paddington, the Jack the Ripper 'Royal Conspiracy' theory suggested that Gull was driven around Whitechapel in a coach by John Netley. The theory, although entertaining, is highly unlikely as by 1888 Gull was in his seventies and had already had at least one stroke.

Sir William Gull (1881)

However this did not stop the film and television industry repeatedly portraying this idea in such films as *Murder by Decree* (where Gull was thinly disguised under the name Sir Thomas Spivey) and *From Hell* starring Johnny Depp. The former film starred Christopher Plummer in the second of his two outings as Sherlock Holmes.

Brook Street has also been home to other famous London residents. Two legendary figures in the field of music lived in adjacent houses albeit at different times. Jimi Hendrix lived at number 23 and the famous composer Handel lived at number 25 from 1723 until his death in 1759[80]. The famous hotel Claridges, which opened in its present form in November 1898[81], can also be found on Brook Street where it connects to Davies Street.

---

[80] The house is now home to the Handel Museum.

[81] Source: Claridges official website.

Scotland Yard

Scotland Yard was founded in 1829 in a street just off Whitehall. The post of Commissioner, which we are accustomed to being occupied by one person, was initially a split role. Sir Charles Rowan (1782 – 1852) and Richard Mayne (1796 – 1868) occupied the posts although the former was recognised as the senior man. In 1850 Rowan retired and Mayne became the senior commissioner with Captain William Hay (1794 – 1855) as second commissioner.

New Scotland Yard building on the Embankment. Since operations moved the building has been renamed Norman Shaw North (2007)

The two men did not enjoy an ideal working relationship but this difficulty ceased when Hay died in 1855. The following year saw the passing of the Police Act in which it was decreed that there would in future be one commissioner with two assistant commissioners. Mayne then remained in sole charge until his death in 1868.

In 1890 Scotland Yard moved to the Victoria Embankment very close to the present day Ministry of Defence (see above picture). At this point it became known as New Scotland Yard. It was to remain in operation from this location until 1967 when operations moved to their present location at 10 Broadway. Curiously the embankment building was not supposed to be there at all. The site was originally supposed to be home to a new opera house designed by a Francis Fowler. The foundation stone for the building had been laid by the then Duke of Edinburgh in December 1875[82]. Sadly, as with so many ambitious projects, a lack of money led to the plans being shelved and the architect Norman Shaw designed the building for the Metropolitan Police instead.

In 1842 the Detective Department had been formed and had introduced the first plain clothed policemen. Thirty-five years later in 1877 this department became involved in what was known as the Turf Fraud Scandal (or Trial of the Detectives). This exposed corruption amongst detectives and led to the department being reorganised and re-launched as the Criminal Investigation Department (or C.I.D.). The job of running this

---

[82] *The Face of London.*

new department fell to Charles Edward Howard Vincent (1849 – 1908).

Charles Edward Howard Vincent – First Director of Criminal Investigation

The position was an awkward one as its incumbent reported directly to the Home Secretary as opposed to the commissioner. This had the effect of creating a force within the force but the situation was resolved in late 1888 when the department began to report to the commissioner.

Vincent is of interest to the Sherlockian by virtue of the date attributed by scholars to the events of *A Study in Scarlet.* This story is said to be set in 1881 which means that Vincent would have been the superior of Inspectors Lestrade and Gregson during the events of that particular case. Vincent left the post in 1884 and was succeeded by James Monro (1838 – 1920).

James Monro – Second head of C.I.D. between 1884 and 1888

Monro served in the post for a shorter period of time than Vincent but his tenure covered a period in which a number of Holmes's cases would have taken place. Monro was also heavily involved in the investigation into the murders of Jack the Ripper and was the sole senior man who did not publish any memoirs of his involvement in that infamous case. It was also during Monro's tenure that the title of the post changed to Assistant Commissioner (Crime).

Monro resigned in September 1888 after a clash with Commissioner Sir Charles Warren. The clash concerned certain police appointments that Warren wished to make and which Monro disagreed with. Unlike Warren he was popular with the then Home Secretary Henry Matthews (1826 – 1913) who promptly moved him to a new post in the Home Office. He was given the title Head of Detectives and was permitted to retain control of the Special Branch[83]. When Warren resigned as Commissioner in November 1888, in the wake of the bad public reaction to Scotland Yard's handling of the Ripper investigation, Monro was appointed by Matthews to succeed him.

Henry Matthews – Home Secretary from 1886 to 1892

[83] The unit of the police concerned with national security. It was originally founded in March 1883 to counter Irish republican groups such as the Fenians.

Over half of the cases investigated by Holmes would have taken place during the tenure of the third head of the C.I.D. This was Sir Robert Anderson (1841 – 1918).

Sir Robert Anderson. Third head of C.I.D from 1888 – 1901

Anderson was a recognised authority on Fenian[84] activities and he became attached to the Home Office as an advisor on political crime. In addition to intelligence gathering he was also the handler for the spy Thomas Miller Beach who had infiltrated the Fenian organisation. He remained involved heavily in the fight against the Fenians until August 1888 when he was appointed as Monro's successor at the C.I.D.

---

[84] The Fenian Brotherhood was a forerunner of the I.R.A. and had very similar goals.

London Embankment 1905 New Scotland Yard can be seen on the left

Anderson resigned his post in 1901 and nine years later published his memoirs entitled *The Lighter Side of My Official Life*. His successor was Edward Richard Henry (1850 – 1931) who on July 1st 1901 established the Metropolitan Police Fingerprint Bureau. This relatively new science was based largely on the work of Sir Francis Galton (1822 – 1911). Galton was by no means the first man to suggest that fingerprints could be used as a means of identification (there had been previous research by Sir William Herschel and Dr Henry Faulds) but his work placed the idea on a more scientific footing which in turn led to it being accepted by the courts as recognisable evidence. Galton and Henry had communicated on the subject when the latter was serving in India as the Inspector-General of Police in Bengal and he had subsequently developed a method of fingerprint classification called the Henry Classification System. This was officially recognised as a means of identifying criminals in India in 1899. It was perhaps fitting therefore, upon his appointment to Scotland Yard, that Henry would be involved in the adoption of the same science for the Metropolis.

The final remark on Henry is that he, like Conan Doyle, was a member of the Athenaeum Club in Pall Mall and even served on its governing committee.

Edward Richard Henry - Fourth head of the C.I.D between 1901 and 1903 (from Spy magazine 1905)

The period covered by Holmes's investigations is generally accepted to be 1874[85] to 1914[86]. This same period saw a massive rise in the number of serving members of the Metropolitan Police. In 1870 records show that there were only 9,160 serving officers. By 1910 this number had risen over one hundred percent to 19,418[87].

Sir Francis Galton – fingerprinting pioneer

---

[85] The Gloria Scott

[86] His Last Bow

[87] Source: *The English Police – A Political and Social History* by Clive Emsley.

Royal College of Surgeons

Plate 31 - Royal College of Surgeons of England (2006)

The Royal College of Surgeons has occupied its present site since 1797 and was granted its present name by Royal Charter in 1843. Its claim on the interest of the Sherlock Holmes fan stems from *The Hound of the Baskervilles*. Doctor Mortimer, who brings the case to Holmes's attention, is a member of the college and during his stay in London with Sir Henry he spends one afternoon at the college's museum.

As Mortimer himself points out to Holmes during their initial interview, he actually should be referred to as 'Mister' rather than 'Doctor'. Members or Fellows of the college highly prize their 'Mister' prefix which is in contrast to some other countries, such as the United States, where surgeons are referred to as 'Doctor'.

Visitors to the college's museum today can view a variety of collections but one that Mortimer could well have viewed during his visit would be the Hunterian collection which the college has held since 1799. One of this collection's most outstanding exhibits is the skeleton of 'The Irish Giant' Charles Byrne (1761 - 1783). His body was purchased soon after his death and stands at seven feet seven inches tall. The collection was amassed by the Scottish surgeon John Hunter (1728 – 1793). He acquired the skeleton of Byrne for his collection against Byrne's last wishes (he wanted to be buried at sea) by bribing a member of the funeral party. He went on to perform a thorough examination of the body and published his findings.

After Hunter's death the government of the day took possession of the collection and gave it to the Royal College of Surgeons after they moved to their present site at Lincoln Inn Fields. As an aside, it is interesting to note that Hunter, like Holmes, had briefly studied at St Bartholomew's Hospital in the mid 1700s. A bust of Hunter can now be seen in Leicester Square where he had a house from 1783 (the same year he acquired Byrne's body).

Today's visitors can view many other interesting collections including one entitled 'Silver and Steel' which is an exhibition of surgical instruments throughout the ages.

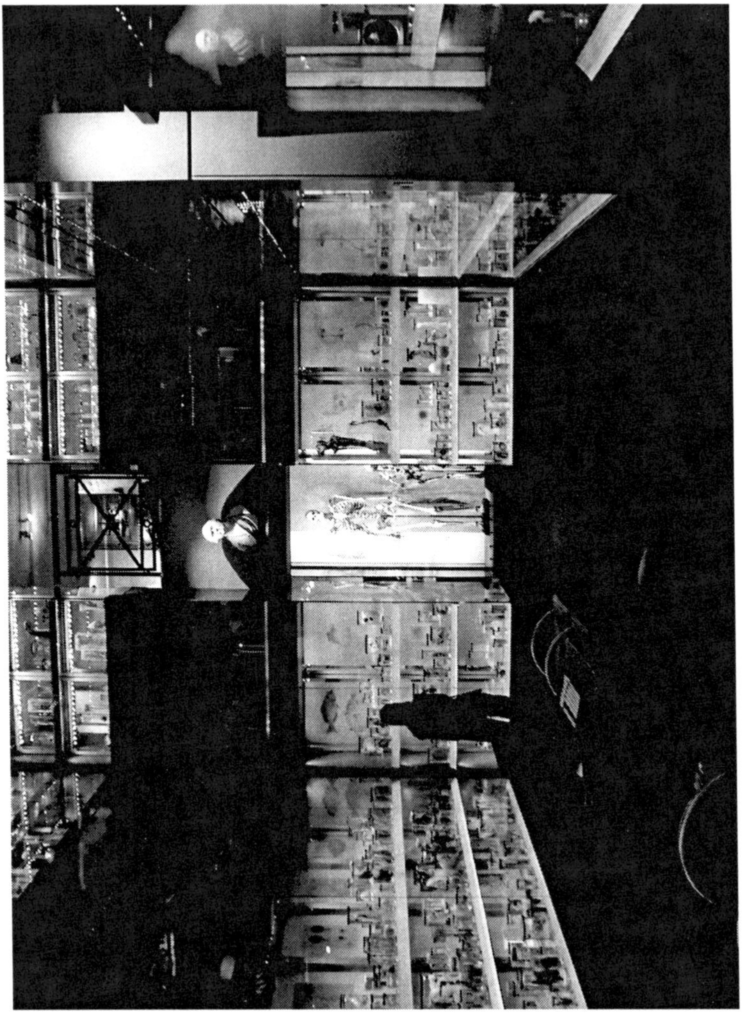

The Hunterian Collection at the Royal College of Surgeons. The skeleton of Charles Byrne can be seen in the centre. Photo by Paul Dean (2007)

Kennington Road

Situated in the borough of Lambeth, Kennington Road was constructed in 1751 after the Westminster Bridge was opened. It formed part of the London to Brighton route and was used by King George IV when he travelled to and from that city. It later became popular as part of the London to Brighton Veteran Car run. The road can also boast a Hollywood connection as Charlie Chaplin lived at number 287 when he was a child.

Charlie Chaplin (1889 – 1977) from 1920 (Aged 31)

Chaplin shares a particularly strong theatrical link with Sherlock Holmes. William Gillette, for his play *Sherlock Holmes – A Drama in Four Acts*, had included the character of Billy the pageboy. When he took the play on tour in 1903 Chaplin was cast as Billy. He was to later repeat the role in Gillette's other play *The Painful Predicament of Sherlock Holmes*. Originally the character only appeared in two Holmes stories[88] (*The Mazarin Stone* and *The Valley of Fear*) but, thanks to Gillette, he gained extra importance and the part was revived in other Holmes adaptations. One of these occurred during Basil Rathbone's series of films when the part was played by Terry Kilburn in *The Adventures of Sherlock Holmes* (1939). Another occurred in Jeremy Brett's Granada series when the part was played by Dean Magri in *The Problem of Thor Bridge* (1991).

For the Holmes fan the road is also interesting as it features in two of the stories. In *The Disappearance of Lady Frances Carfax* the coffin in which Lady Frances is almost buried comes from Stimson & Co. a firm of undertakers on Kennington Road.

The other connection is that this road is described as the home of the shop belonging to Morse Hudson, a purveyor of pictures and statues. It is from this shop that the eponymous statues from *The Six Napoleons* are bought prior to being sought out and smashed. No less than two meet their end in Kennington Road. The very first to be destroyed is actually in Morse Hudson's shop and the second is smashed in the home of a Dr Barnicot whose home was also on Kennington Road.

---

[88] According to our usual sources these two stories are set fifteen years apart. *The Valley of Fear* is said to be set in 1888 and *The Mazarin Stone* in 1903 (Klinger's dates). Therefore it is hard to see how the same Billy could still be Holmes's pageboy.

Kennington Road – Here we see the more retail end where it is likely that Morse Hudson would have had his shop (2008)

Morse Hudson's shop and Stimson & Co. Undertakers are likely to have been situated in what might be described as the retail end of Kennington Road which is south of the crossing with Kennington Lane[89] and more towards the Oval cricket ground. The road continues north of Kennington Lane where it becomes more residential and it is in this stretch of the road that it is likely that Dr Barnicot would have lived.

---

[89] Kennington Lane was travelled by Holmes and Watson in their pursuit of Jonathan Small in *The Sign of Four*.

The more residential section of Kennington Road (2008) Dr Barnicot would most likely have lived in one of these houses.

The Three Norwoods

Outside of central London, South Norwood has the strongest claim on the attention of fans of both Sherlock Holmes and Arthur Conan Doyle. Despite this the area's residents seem to have very little interest in the connection.

12 Tennison Road – The English Heritage Plaque, which was erected in 1973, can just be seen on the right (2008)

It is common for sites of interest to be signposted but this is not the case for Conan Doyle's former house at 12 Tennison Road. This could well be down to a desire to discourage visitors as its present day use is as a residential facility for people suffering from autism which is a purpose quite apt for the former home of a one-time practicing doctor.

12 Tennison Road during Conan Doyle's residence (Strand Magazine August 1892)

During his residence in the area between 1891 and 1894 Conan Doyle wrote approximately one third of all the Sherlock Holmes stories. Among those written in South Norwood were *The Blue Carbuncle* and *The Speckled Band*. The latter, as we have seen, was Conan Doyle's favourite Sherlock Holmes story[90]. In November 1891, according to his own letters to his mother, Conan Doyle first admitted to the idea of killing Holmes. Less than two years later in April 1893 he wrote *The Final Problem* (published December 1893) in which Sherlock Holmes did indeed meet his end – albeit temporarily. So it would not necessarily be an exaggeration to say that South Norwood can lay claim to being the home of the most famous literary murder in history.

Despite living in South Norwood, Conan Doyle only featured the area in one Holmes story and even then it was implied rather than being explicit. The story concerned was *The Norwood Builder*. The majority of events were actually set in Lower Norwood (today referred to as West Norwood – see later) and the link to South Norwood lay solely in the fact that the villain of the story took an express train from a station in Norwood to London Bridge. This is only possible from Norwood Junction Station in South Norwood[91].

The other story that may have a link is *The Sign of Four* and it concerns South Norwood police station. The Metropolitan Police took possession of the site in 1873[92] and a station still stands today. The events of *The Sign of Four* are set some fifteen years after the acquisition of the site and this is one of the

---

[90] The choice was disclosed by Conan Doyle in a list of twelve stories revealed in 1927.

[91] Although the station is called Norwood Junction today it has only been known as such since 1955. Since it opened in 1839 it has had four names and was known simply as Norwood Station at the time of *The Norwood Builder* and *The Sign of Four*.

[92] Source: Metropolitan Police Official Website.

possible police stations that Thaddeus Sholto came to, at Sherlock Holmes's behest, in order to fetch the police after the discovery of his brother's body at their late father's house in Upper Norwood.

Conan Doyle (right) and fellow author Robert Barr outside 12 Tennison Road in 1894. Two years earlier Barr had written a Holmes parody called The Adventures of Sherlaw Kombs (picture courtesy of Phil Cornell)

Bernard Davies, in his magnum opus *Holmes and Watson Country – Travels in Search of Solutions*, makes an excellent case for Kilravock House being the model for the Sholto residence - Pondicherry Lodge[93]. This house (which has since been converted into flats) sits on the border of Upper and South Norwood and has at various times been regarded as being one side or the other depending on the official boundary of the day (it is today regarded as being in South Norwood but would have been classed as being in Upper Norwood during the 1880s).

Kilravock House (2008) identified as a candidate for the 'real' Pondicherry Lodge by Bernard Davies

[93] Please see bibliography for full details of Mr Davies' book.

If this were indeed the house it would lend weight to South Norwood being the visited station where Athelney Jones was present[94]. However it is only a possibility as there are other contenders as we shall see later.

South Norwood Police station (2008)

Jack Tracey, in his book *Sherlock Holmes – The Published Apocrypha*, suggested another link between South Norwood and Holmes / Doyle. The story goes that in 1898, five years after the 'death' of Holmes, the American stage actor William Gillette composed a stage play featuring Sherlock Holmes. This, as we have already mentioned in our look at the Lyceum Theatre, was

[94] Jack Tracy, in his book *The Encyclopaedia Sherlockiana*, expresses his preference for South Norwood Police Station.

based on a play originally composed by Conan Doyle. Before its debut in the United States Gillette travelled to England in order to meet Conan Doyle and receive his blessing. Conan Doyle arrived at the station to meet Gillette and the latter, for a joke, had dressed up as Sherlock Holmes. When he stepped down from the train dressed in, amongst other things, a deerstalker hat Conan Doyle was naturally rather taken aback. However the event was an excellent ice-breaker and the two men became firm friends.

Station Road, South Norwood 1905. The station can be seen at the end of the road.

Regrettably this story, although true in every other respect, has no connection with South Norwood. Tracey states that Conan Doyle met Gillette at South Norwood station (Norwood Junction – see above) but this cannot be the case. Conan Doyle had moved out of the area four years earlier and was living in his house Undershaw near Hindhead in Surrey. The nearest rail station to Hindhead is situated in Haslemere, approximately three miles away, and it is here that Conan Doyle and Gillette were most likely to meet.

Norwood Junction Station (2008) – The view is towards central London. It is from here that Jonas Oldacre would have caught his train to London Bridge to meet John Hector McFarlane. Platform three is today where the express trains to London Bridge depart from.

The possible argument that Conan Doyle travelled to South Norwood to meet Gillette is unlikely in the extreme as the two stations are not on the same route and Conan Doyle would have had to change trains several times. Assuming that Gillette was staying at a central London hotel it would be most probable that he travelled to Haslemere from London Waterloo. This journey today takes approximately forty minutes. This hypothesis is backed up by John Dickson Carr in his book *The Life of Sir Arthur Conan Doyle* in which he states that Conan Doyle met Gillette at a station a few miles from Undershaw. Any further doubt is dispelled by Conan Doyle's own letters where, writing from Undershaw, he states that Gillette is going to be in England

and that he hopes to get him 'down here' for a meeting. The implied location is clear.

A close up view of Norwood Junction Station c1900 – Courtesy of Croydon Local Studies Library

Conan Doyle's son Kingsley was born during his residence in South Norwood. The date of his birth was November 15th 1892 and his baptism took place at St Marks Church on December 22nd. The ceremony was performed by Stuart Yardley and Conan Doyle's occupation was listed as 'Gentleman'. The full name given to his son was Arthur Alleyne Kingsley Conan Doyle but he was known as Kingsley. Sadly he was to die from pneumonia in October 1917 which he contracted after being wounded at the battle of the Somme in 1916.

Louise Conan Doyle (died 1906) was mother to Conan Doyle's first two children Marie Louise (born 1889) and Kingsley (born 1892). Kingsley was the only child of Conan Doyle to be born in South Norwood.

Today there are several churches in South Norwood and visitors to the area may be confused by the fact that the Holy Innocents church is closer to Conan Doyle's house than St Marks. The explanation for this is simple. The Holy Innocents church was actually built between 1894 and 1895[95] so did not exist at the time[96].

The man for whom South Norwood has the most regard and one of the reasons that Conan Doyle is relatively ignored is another non-native by the name of William Stanley. He arrived in 1867 and threw himself into local life founding a technical college in 1907, serving as a school governor and arranging the construction of a community hall which is still in use today. Such was the high regard in which he was held, the residents arranged for the erection of a clock tower in honour of Mr and Mrs Stanley's 50th wedding anniversary.

The honours for Stanley do not end there. More recently the well known British Pub chain J.D. Wetherspoon opened an outlet in South Norwood High Street and named it The William Stanley. In common with many pubs of the chain the inside contains many pictures depicting the local area of the early 1900s and there are framed pictures of notable people with details of their connections to the area and their achievements. Significantly, Conan Doyle is not amongst the people mentioned[97].

---

[95] Source: Diocese of Southwark Website

[96] St Marks church was built much earlier in 1852 and the architect was a G.H. Lewis.

[97] The present author is attempting to get this oversight corrected at the time of writing.

St Marks Church, South Norwood (2008). Conan Doyle's son Kingsley was baptised here in December 1892

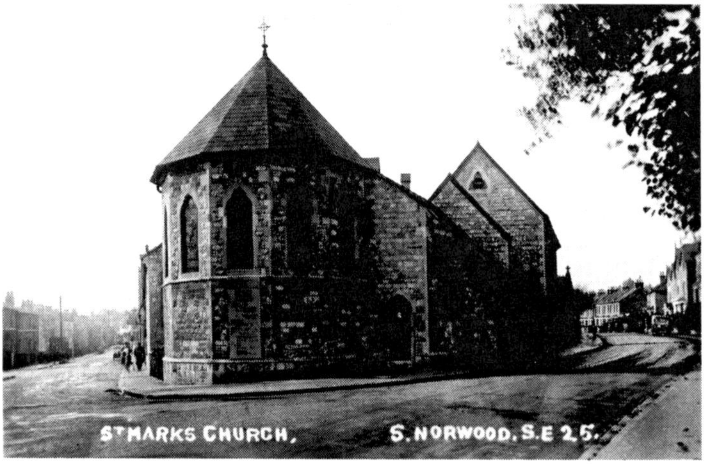

St Marks Church (1905) Courtesy of Croydon Local Studies Library

The interior of St Marks Church (1905) Courtesy of Croydon Local Studies Library

The unveiling of the Stanley Clock tower (1907) Courtesy of Croydon Local Studies Library

The repainted clock tower today (2008)

Despite the area's dedication to William Stanley, Conan Doyle does have a couple of sites that refer to his connection to the area apart from his former house. Approximately five minutes walk from the Stanley clock tower there is a Doyle road. This road was originally called Farley Road but was changed some time after the end of the Second World War in order to avoid it being confused with another Farley Road situated three miles away. Whether it was renamed after Conan Doyle or not is open to debate but some local sources are certain that it was.

Even closer than Doyle Road there is a mosaic which can be found under the railway bridge that crosses Portland Road. The mosaic was erected in July 1997 and commemorates the cultural, agricultural, industrial and literary aspects of the area.

Conan Doyle's name as featured on the mosaic under Norwood Junction Railway Bridge crossing Portland Road (2008)

In Conan Doyle's day South Norwood was part of the county of Surrey but it was incorporated into Greater London in 1965 as part of the Local Government act of 1963. The area today comes under the control of the borough of Croydon and is considered one of the most deprived areas of the borough. In view of this situation it is odd that the area does not do more to maximise its connections to Conan Doyle and Sherlock Holmes and thus put itself on the tourist map. It is conceivable that local residents baulk at the idea of attracting hoards of tourists but they would provide a much needed cash injection to the area and perhaps encourage other mainstream retailers and thus more employment.

Stanley Halls where the mosaic was assembled (2008)

The sign for Doyle Road, South Norwood (2008)

Doyle Road looking north (2008)

Upper Norwood's principal claim on the attention of the Sherlockian lies in its connection to the story *The Sign of Four.* In this story, arguably the most famous Holmes adventure after *The Hound of the Baskervilles*, Major Sholto and his sons live in Pondicherry Lodge in Upper Norwood[98]. It is also here that Bartholomew Sholto meets his end at the hands of Jonathan Small's ally Tonga.

View from Centre Hill towards Westow Hill, Upper Norwood c1890. The original Gipsy Hill Police Station was down the road to the left.

[98] As just discussed, the potential candidate Kilravock House is now considered to be in South Norwood.

Approximately the same viewpoint (2008)

The area was quite a wealthy one and Church Road (as shown below) was a very popular address for stockbrokers due to its proximity to no less than three stations that provided routes to London Bridge (and hence the City of London financial institutions). The three stations still exist today and are Gipsy Hill (opened 1856), Anerley (opened 1839) and Crystal Palace (opened 1854).

A natural question to ask is why Sholto chose Upper Norwood in which to live. Given that he lived in fear of vengeance it is certain that he wanted to live somewhere where he could more easily guard himself. Despite how close it seems to London now, Upper Norwood (like South Norwood) was part of Surrey until the Local Government Act of 1963. It would have been a lot less built up in the 1880s and hence it was possible for Sholto to purchase a house that was walled off within its own grounds. The story makes clear his disinclination to use the Agra treasure and that he much preferred to possess it rather than spend it. However he must have utilised some of it, despite his statement to the contrary, in order to purchase his house, pay his staff and educate his sons (an army pension would certainly have been insufficient and he already had many debts). The most obvious solution is that some of the treasure was invested, perhaps on the stock market (Sholto was a gambler after all), after the purchase of Pondicherry Lodge in order to generate an income which enabled him to support his establishment.

Church Road, Upper Norwood c1900

Such an investment would need management and no doubt required Sholto to visit the City on occasion to do so. Hence he chose a location South of London and close to a rail line into

London Bridge in order that he could access the City easily[99]. Upper Norwood is also the site of the second of the three police stations to which Thaddeus Sholto may have come when sent to fetch the police upon the discovery of his brother's body. We have already looked at Bernard Davies' theory as to the location of Pondicherry Lodge and hence the likelihood of South Norwood station's candidature. However if you choose not to accept this theory it opens up the debate about which police station was the one visited (out of South Norwood, Upper Norwood and West Norwood) and makes things very difficult. The problem arises from a remark made by Holmes to Watson after they despatch Thaddeus to fetch the police. Holmes tells Watson that they have half an hour before the police arrive. So how does he arrive at this estimate?

Presumably it is based on the time it would take Thaddeus to travel to and from the station and explain the crime when he arrived. Holmes does not specify which station Thaddeus should go to (he simply instructs him to 'drive down to the station') so it is logical to suppose that he would head for the nearest. However if you abandon the earlier theory you have no immediate way of determining the nearest station. When Inspector Athelney Jones subsequently arrives on the scene he appears to be aware of most of the events leading up to the discovery (even if he does draw inaccurate conclusions). This implies that a good part of Thaddeus's time was spent explaining the full situation. This naturally leaves less time for travelling and implies a short

---

[99] If Kilravock House was indeed the model for Pondicherry Lodge the closest stations would have been at Thornton Heath (opened 1862), Selhurst (opened 1865) and Norwood Junction (opened 1839). The latter, as we know, provided express trains.

distance to the station. This does not entirely lay the matter to rest however as Jones may have interrogated Thaddeus in the cab on the way to Pondicherry Lodge.

Moving on from *The Sign of Four,* unquestionably the main attraction of the area was the Crystal Palace which had been relocated from Hyde Park and had been open since 1854, a mere five years prior to Conan Doyle's birth. Twenty years later he would actually visit as part of a trip to London[100].

10 Gipsy Hill. At the time of The Sign of Four this building was the Upper Norwood police station (2008)

[100] Source: *Conan Doyle: The Man Who Created Sherlock Holmes* by Andrew Lycett.

A short distance from the old Gipsy Hill Police Station is Woodland Hill. In this immediate area there was an orphanage run by one Charles Chapman. Its claim on the interest of the reader lies in the fact that one of this orphanage's residents was a Kate Russell. In 1879 she married Dr. George Turnavine Budd (Conan Doyle's first medical partner) at a registry office in the Strand. At the age of seventeen she was not legally able to marry and was forced to lie in order for the ceremony to proceed[101].

Crystal Palace late 1800s

Anerley is just south of Crystal Palace and its main claim on the attention of the Sherlock Holmes fan arises from its appearance in the story *The Norwood Builder*. A great many places in the Sherlock Holmes stories were made up by Conan Doyle and

---

[101] *On the Trail of Arthur Conan Doyle* by Brian Pugh and Paul Spiring.

theories as to their real locations abound. However there is no such ambiguity with Anerley. In *The Norwood Builder*, John Hector McFarlane explains his story to Holmes upon his arrival at Baker Street and states clearly that he had spent the previous night in the Anerley Arms.

The Anerley Arms[102] was one of the many buildings occupying two areas known as the Anerley Estate (developed 1851) and the Anerley Station Estate (developed 1853). The area consisted primarily of shops with first floor flats and it swiftly became something of a commercial centre. The Anerley Arms was not the first business to occupy its site. It was built after the demolition of the hotel and tearooms that were adjacent to the Anerley Gardens. The gardens were a major leisure site (opened in 1841) and in addition to the hotel and tearooms there were a band stand and a maze. The gardens also encompassed a section of the old Croydon canal and this was used for pleasure boating. Sadly the arrival of the Crystal Palace caused too much competition and the gardens began to lose visitors. They finally closed in 1868 and this was when the tearooms were demolished and replaced with the present public house.[103] With *The Norwood Builder* being said to have been set in 1894[104] the Anerley Arms would have been a relatively new pub having been open only twenty-six years by the time McFarlane stayed

---

[102] It is interesting to note that in the 1977 edition of Jack Tracy's *The Encyclopaedia Sherlockiana*, an asterisk precedes the entry for the Anerley Arms. This denotes that the entry is fictitious. Presumably Tracy had not been able to verify its existence at the time.

[103] Source: *Ideal Homes: Suburbia in focus.*

[104] Dakin and Klinger agree on this date.

there (assuming that the pub opened in the same year the tearooms were demolished).

Anerley Arms in 2008

The Anerley Arms today is a relatively quiet place being some small distance from the main retail area of Crystal Palace. With the exception of some all too modern features the interior is very much as it would have been in late Victorian times and it is quite possible to imagine what it would have been like filled with Victorian customers who were perhaps waiting for a train or paying a visit for a quick post-commute drink on the way home from the City of London.

West Norwood has only been known as such since 1885. Prior to this it was known as Lower Norwood. The name simply referred to the fact that the area was at a lower altitude to the other Norwood districts. In 1880 the first moves to change the name were taken. The reasons for the change are unclear but perhaps it was felt that the prefix 'Lower' implied a lower class of people or standard of living to Upper Norwood.

Norwood Road, West Norwood early 1900s

The name change was by no means a universally popular idea. Many businesses opposed it due to the costs involved in legally changing their names. Similarly the legal position of large numbers of title deeds containing 'Lower Norwood' was a cause of concern to some residents[105]. Despite this the name change went ahead.

In the late 1700s Lower Norwood contained a relatively small number of fully detached houses or villas. They were

---

[105] *Story of Norwood* by JB Wilson.

usually occupied by the better off as the working class were generally to be found in South Norwood. The arrival in 1854 of the Crystal Palace in Upper Norwood changed the housing situation beyond recognition. The increase in population that this and the improved rail links brought to the area led to many of the residential properties being demolished to make way for newer terraced and semi-detached dwellings that could accommodate more people in the same space[106]. In fact the arrival of the Crystal Palace vastly improved the amenities for both Upper and Lower Norwood as the tenfold increase in population that occurred between 1851 and 1901 led to proper supplies of water and gas coming to the area as it became worthwhile for companies to invest in the necessary infrastructure. Prior to this the water in Lower Norwood had all come from wells.

Conan Doyle would certainly have travelled through this area whenever he travelled from South Norwood to London. In fact it is not unreasonable to suppose that he may have house hunted here before finally ending up in Tennison Road. His knowledge of the area, however it was obtained, certainly inspired one of his Sherlock Holmes stories.

In *The Norwood Builder* Jonas Oldacre is a resident of Lower Norwood and it is here that he meets, at his home, with John Hector McFarlane as part of his plot to frame the latter for his murder. The curious thing to note is that Lower Norwood is referred to as such throughout the story. By the time the story was published it had been many years since the area had been renamed to West Norwood[107].

---

[106] British History Online.

[107] According to many sources the date of the story's setting is 1894 and it was published in 1903. Both dates are some time after the

As we have already seen, Oldacre took his train to London Bridge from South Norwood. This is implied by Holmes's deduction that Oldacre's handwritten will was written on an express train (which are only available from Norwood Junction in South Norwood). However we need to ask why he did this. West Norwood got its railway station in 1856 and it is true that originally it was on the line that served Victoria Station. Therefore, on that basis, it made sense for him to take a train from South Norwood as this was the most direct means of reaching London Bridge. However, according to the 1897 *Royal Atlas of England and Wales*, it was possible to reach London Bridge from West Norwood. It may well have taken longer and required some changes but it was possible. So the only reason for going all the way to South Norwood for a train was to get an express that made few stops (in fact only stopping at New Cross en route to London Bridge).

However, one has to wonder what Oldacre's hurry was as no doubt most of his nefarious plans had been made well in advance

---

renaming to West Norwood. This was the second story to have input from Conan Doyle's friend Bertram Fletcher Robinson (see section on Liverpool Street Station). As we saw, the idea for using the wax impression of a thumbprint as a means of incriminating someone came from Robinson. However one has to wonder why Conan Doyle purchased the idea from him at all. At the time he paid out for this idea Sherlock Holmes had been dead at the foot of the Reichenbach Falls for eight years and there were as yet no plans to resurrect him. So why did Conan Doyle purchase an idea that was only really suitable for a crime novel? Perhaps he was already toying with the idea of Holmes's return or maybe he had an idea for a non-Holmes story where the idea could be used.

and a slightly longer train journey would have allowed him more time to draft his infamous will. Perhaps Conan Doyle wrote the story this way purely to set the scene for Holmes's subsequent deduction.

Jonas Oldacre is scared out of hiding place in his Lower Norwood House in The Norwood Builder

One of the most famous (or infamous) residents of West Norwood during the life of Conan Doyle was Sir Hiram Stevens Maxim (1840 – 1916). Between 1883 and 1885 he patented the design of the machine gun that bears his name. Originally an American, Maxim became a British subject and it was in his West Norwood home that he further developed his design. His gun had been initially rejected by the United States military but was welcomed by the British armed forces. It was later to be sold to other European countries and was used to devastating effect during the First World War. Upon his death Maxim was buried in West Norwood cemetery[108].

West Norwood is also the last of the three possible locations for the police station visited by Thaddeus Sholto in *The Sign of Four*. This station would have been the closest of the three to London and the main aspect in its favour comes from Athelney Jones. When he arrives on the scene at Pondicherry Lodge, he mentions that he was 'in Norwood' on another case. West Norwood stands alone in the fact that it is often referred to simply as Norwood without a prefix. Of course another interpretation was that Jones was simply grouping all the districts together under one heading for convenience.

---

[108] The Norwood Society

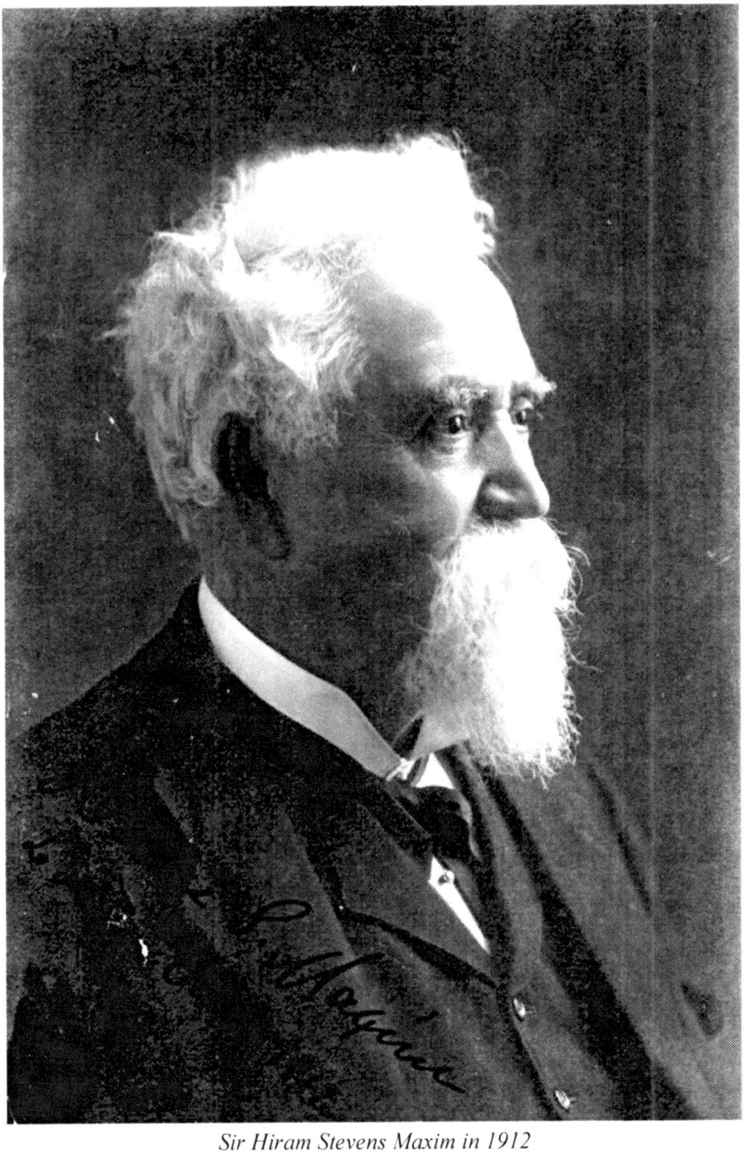

Sir Hiram Stevens Maxim in 1912

Croydon

Croydon is built on the site of an ancient Saxon settlement. During the middle ages it was a centre for charcoal production, leather and brewing. Centuries later it was also the site of the world's first horse drawn railway which was used to transport goods to and from Wandsworth. This was to subsequently become an important mode of transport which over time facilitated the transformation of Croydon into a London commuter town.

The increasing popularity of Brighton in the late eighteenth and early nineteenth centuries (thanks in no small part to the Prince Regent – later George IV) led to Croydon becoming an important stop for stage coaches en route to the coast from London. In 1839 Croydon's transport connections were improved further with the opening of the London and Croydon Railway. The route started from West Croydon station and ran all the way to London Bridge. This had the effect of making Croydon an attractive place to live for the Victorian middle class who were drawn to the leafy suburb with its swift access to the City of London. In the late 1880s it was possible to reach the City of London from Croydon in around fifteen to twenty minutes which is not much different from the journey time today.

The rapid population expansion that the railway brought to Croydon generated its own set of problems. The overcrowding in the older parts of the town caused a series of public health issues.

These became of such concern that in 1849 Croydon got a local board of health which set to work improving matters with the construction of proper sewers and a reservoir. Croydon was one of the first towns to have such a body looking after its health.

1860 saw the opening of a rail route to London Victoria but this was very much the less important line. West London at this stage was the location for entertainment rather than office space. This situation was to remain the same until the early twentieth century. On Sunday mornings the train companies operated what became known as a 'church break'. During this period no trains operated. The idea behind this was to discourage people from travelling when they should be in church.[109]

Today Croydon is approximately a fifteen minute car or bus journey from South Norwood and it is certainly possible that Conan Doyle visited during the period from mid 1891 to 1894 when he was resident in Tennison Road. What is certain is that one of the Sherlock Holmes stories, *The Cardboard Box*, was largely set in Croydon. This is the story where, due to a mistake, a Miss Susan Cushing receives a box containing two severed ears. She is described as living in Cross Street but a road of this exact name does not exist. There is however a Cross Road which may well have been the road Conan Doyle meant.

If this is indeed the road that Conan Doyle was thinking of it answers the question as to which of Croydon's stations Holmes and Watson travelled to in order to meet Inspector Lestrade and visit Miss Cushing.

---

[109] *Croydon: The Story of a Hundred Years.*

Cross Road, Croydon in 1996. Courtesy of Croydon Local Studies Library

The Cardboard Box is widely accepted by scholars to be set in 1888 (it was published in 1893). At this time there were two railway stations in proximity to Cross Road. West Croydon Station and East Croydon (opened July 12th 1841). Contemporary maps clearly show that the latter is the closer to Cross Road. There are today considerable numbers of express or fast trains from London to East Croydon that only stop once or twice on their way south. We already know from our look at Norwood Junction that the situation was very much the same in the late 1800s. Knowing that Holmes was not a man who wasted time we can be reasonably certain that it would have been an express train to this station that he and Watson used. If we then add to this the fact that in the story the journey from the station to Miss Cushing's house is described as a 'walk of five minutes' it becomes even more likely that Cross Road is the Cross Street of the story.

A train arrives at East Croydon Station (1909). The picture very much represents the station as Holmes and Watson would have seen it upon their arrival in Croydon - Courtesy of Croydon Local Studies Library

Lestrade, Holmes and Watson examine the severed ears at the house of Susan Cushing in Croydon in The Cardboard Box (1893)

East Croydon Station (2008)

East Croydon Station in 1905, thirteen years after The Cardboard Box was published in the Strand. The main building essentially remained unchanged until the 1990s when it was rebuilt. Courtesy of Croydon Local Studies Library

Conclusion

So we have reached the end of our look at Holmes and Conan Doyle's London. A major city such as London is forever on the move and it is perfectly possible, when writing a book such as this, to be overtaken by events.

The closure of the Café Royal on Regent Street is a perfect example of this continual change. At the time I originally wrote my section on Regent Street, the Café Royal was still a working business. As I write these lines the Café has been shut for several days and by the time you read this its contents will have been auctioned by Bonhams auctioneers. Fortunately for me this change occurred in time for me to alter my text but who is to say what else may change after this book makes it into your hands.

My thanks go out once again to all those who helped me in the production of this book. I hope you all like it.

APD.

Bibliography

Baring-Gould, W.S. Sherlock Holmes - A biography of the world's first consulting detective. Published by Panther. ISBN 586-04260-1

Baring-Gould, W.S. The Annotated Sherlock Holmes. Published by John Murray. ISBN 0517502917

Carr, John Dickson. The Life of Sir Arthur Conan Doyle. Published by Carroll & Graff. ISBN 07867 1234 1

Clunn, Harold P. The Face of London. Published by Spring Books.

Dakin, D. Martin. A Sherlock Holmes Commentary. Published by David & Charles. ISBN 0-7153-5493-0

Davies, Bernard. Holmes and Watson Country: Travels in Search of Solutions. Published by The Sherlock Holmes Society of London.

Doyle, Arthur Conan. The Penguin Complete Sherlock Holmes. Published by Penguin. ISBN 0-14-005694-7

Emsley, Clive. The English Police: A Political and Social History. Published by Longman. ISBN 0582257689

Foley, Charles. Stashower, Daniel. Lellenberg Jon. Arthur Conan Doyle - A Life in Letters. Published by Harper Collins. ISBN 978-0-00-724759-2

Green, Richard Lancelyn. Conan Doyle of Wimpole Street. Published by The Arthur Conan Doyle Society. ISBN 1 899060 02 2

Green, Richard Lancelyn. Letters to Sherlock Holmes. Penguin Books. ISBN 0-1400-70354

Holroyd, James Edward. Baker Street By-Ways. Published by George Allen & Unwin

Jackson, Lee. A Dictionary of Victorian London. Published by Anthem Press. ISBN 1 84331 230 1

Klinger. Leslie S. The New Annotated Sherlock Holmes Volumes 1 & 2. Published by Norton. ISBN 0-393-05916-2

Klinger. Leslie S. The New Annotated Sherlock Holmes Volumes 3. Published by Norton. ISBN 0-393-05800-X

Lycett, Andrew. Conan Doyle - The Man Who Created Sherlock Holmes. Published by Weidenfeld & Nicolson. ISBN 0297848526

Machmichael, J. Holden. The Story of Charing Cross, Published by Chatto & Windus.

Pointer, Michael. The Pictorial History of Sherlock Holmes. Published by WH Smith. ISBN 0861248546

Pugh, Brian and Spiring Paul. Bertram Fletcher Robinson: A Footnote to the Hound of the Baskervilles. MX Publishing. ISBN 1-904312-411

Pugh, Brian and Spiring Paul. On the Trail of Arthur Conan Doyle: An Illustrated Devon Tour. Book Guild Limited. ISBN 1-84624198-7

Tracy, Jack. The Encyclopaedia Sherlockiana. New English Library. ISBN 450-040-275.

Tracy, Jack. Sherlock Holmes - The Published Apocrypha. Gaslight Publications. ISBN 0-93-446824-9

Various Authors. Arthur Conan Doyle (Crowborough) Establishment 2008 Birthday File.

Various Authors. Croydon: The Story of a Hundred Years. Published by the Croydon Natural History & Scientific Society Limited.

Various Authors. The Further Adventures of Sherlock Holmes. Published by Penguin. ISBN 0-14-00.7907-6

Viney, Charles. Sherlock Holmes in London. Published by Equation. ISBN 1853361321

Wilson, J.B. The Story of Norwood. Published by London Borough of Lambeth. ISBN 0950189332

Index

Also from MX Publishing:

Brian W. Pugh and Paul R. Spiring

Bertram Fletcher Robinson

A Footnote to the Hound of the Baskervilles

Also from MX Publishing:

Alistair Duncan

Eliminate the Impossible

An Examination of the World of

Sherlock Holmes on Page and Screen

Printed in the United Kingdom by
Lightning Source UK Ltd., Milton Keynes
136773UK00001B/118-165/P

9 781904 312505